FISH

GREGORY MONE

FISH

SCHOLASTIC PRESS
New York

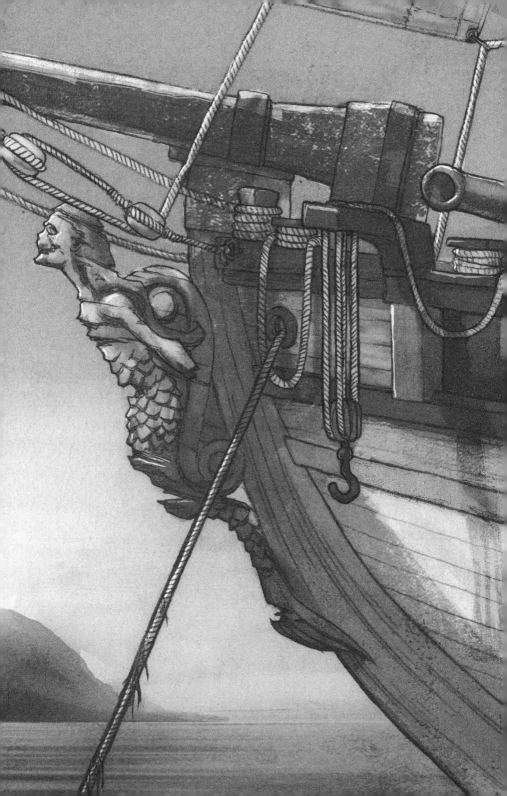

Library of Congress Cataloging-in-Publication Data

Mone, Gregory.
    Fish / Gregory Mone. — 1st ed.
      p. cm.
    Summary: Eleven-year-old Fish, seeking a way to help his family
financially, becomes a reluctant cabin boy on a pirate ship, where he soon
makes friends — and enemies — and is asked to help decipher clues that
might lead to a legendary treasure.
    ISBN-13: 978-0-545-11632-9 — ISBN-10: 0-545-11632-5 [1. Pirates —
Fiction. 2. Conduct of life — Fiction. 3. Ciphers — Fiction. 4. Buried
treasure — Fiction.] I. Title.
    PZ7.M742Fis 2010
    [Fic] — dc22

                                                  2009037533

        10 9 8 7 6 5 4 3 2 1   10 11 12 13 14
                    Printed in the U.S.A.   23
                    First edition, April 2010

To Clare, Eleanor, and the
Orient Point Treasure Hunting Society

CONTENTS

FISH ON A FARM

The rain had been falling heavily for weeks. The rivers could hold no more water; they flooded farms and towns and houses all across the lush, green island called Ireland. And the Reidy home was no exception. Several inches of water had gathered on the floor of the cottage on the day Maurice, the fifth child of Fergal and Brigid Reidy, was born. Years later, when Fergal learned that his son had chosen a life at sea, he would think of those floods. He would wonder if the boy felt at home on the open ocean because he'd entered into this world surrounded by water.

The floods stopped eventually, and Maurice grew up in a dry and increasingly crowded home. Patrick was the oldest child, followed by Michael, Mary, and Conor, then Maurice, Roisin, Kathleen, Patricia, and, finally, the youngest, Maureen. The Reidys were farmers, and the boys were expected to help Fergal in the fields, but from an early age it became clear that Maurice wasn't much good at the work. His brothers were twice as fast, far more thorough, and only too happy to remind him of his deficiencies, often when their father was within range. They enjoyed torturing him in other ways, too, but he had a friend and ally in Roisin. If Michael or Conor snuck a worm into his shoe, dropped a pebble in his soup, or dribbled some mud into his milk, she'd be the one to warn him. And whenever Queen Mary, as they called the oldest sister, gave Roisin one too many orders, Maurice would help her with the extra chore.

As for his nickname, Fish — he earned it on a warm autumn morning. The Reidy boys had just finished marching across three farms and through a wood to a clear and cold lake. They called it Outhouse Lake because Michael would always relieve himself along the shore just moments after they'd arrived. They would walk there once a week to bathe, always remaining in the shallows since none of them knew how to swim.

As usual, his brothers started fighting the moment they stepped into the water, and, as usual, Fish considered trying to stop them. He did not like it when people fought, but he also knew there was such a thing as harmless roughhousing. Michael and Patrick were the chief troublemakers, but their battles were waged in good fun. Conor, on the other hand, was short-tempered and quick to transform an innocent scrap into a bruising brawl.

On that particularly warm morning, they were wading out into the water when Michael pushed Conor from behind. Conor fell but returned to his feet quickly, only to find Michael and Patrick laughing. Immediately he burst into a rage. He grabbed a stone from the bottom of the lake and prepared to swing at Michael's head. Fish threw himself at Conor, grasping for the arm with the stone. Conor, angrier than ever, picked up his younger brother and hurled him out toward the middle of the lake.

Fish didn't fly far, but it proved to be far enough, past an unseen ledge where the shallow water ended and the deep part of the lake began. He tried to plant his feet on the bottom, thinking they'd land in the silt of the lake, but they found only water. He began to sink.

He heard Michael, Patrick, and Conor all shouting. And then, as he slipped below the surface, he stopped hearing anything at all. He closed his mouth, sank further, and, when he thought the lake was going to swallow him for good, he learned how to swim.

Unexpectedly, he felt comfortable below the surface, enveloped by the lake. He started to relax, felt his palms pushing the water. When he moved his palms down, he moved up. When he moved them to the right, he spun to the left. He reached high above his head, pulled his hands down as hard as he could, past his waist, and his body shot upward. The sunlight shone through the surface of the lake; he kept pulling. Finally, just as it felt like his chest was closing in, he broke through the surface and sucked in an enormous gulp of air.

At this point, the average child probably would have headed directly back to shore, into the shallows, and run straight home for his mother. Maurice? He smiled, laughed, cheered, and stroked right out into the middle of the lake.

From then on, whenever they returned to Outhouse Lake, Maurice would swim and splash and dive for as long as his parents would allow. His father came with them on occasion and thought it strange the way his son was so comfortable out in the depths. But he had no comment on his behavior; he merely grunted. His mother, on the other hand, found it downright unacceptable. "I'm trying to raise a man," she'd yell, "not a fish!"

That is how he acquired his name. Of course, the name had little to do with his appearance: He had no gills and no fins. He was a skinny kid, with short, straight, brown hair, hazel eyes shielded by long lashes, slightly oversized front teeth, and a small nose dotted with faded brown freckles. In his looks, therefore, he was very much a boy, yet his brothers and sisters began calling him Fish, not Maurice, and it felt natural. He was at home in the water, not on the farm.

This discovery turned out to be an important one, given the fact that two years later, thanks to a dead horse, a mildly mysterious uncle, and a crafty thief, he would find himself on a pirate ship, leaving solid ground behind him for good.

THE PIRATE THIEF

Early one fall evening, when Fish was eleven years old, Fergal slumped into the cottage and announced, "Shamrock is dead."

Shamrock was the family horse and arguably its most valuable member, after Fergal and Brigid. Without Shamrock, they'd barely be able to grow enough to feed themselves. One of the children, Fergal declared, would have to work in the city to send money home and help the family. Patrick volunteered — he was the oldest — but he was too good of a farmhand to lose. There was really no question of who would have to go, given the fact that he was miserable at farming, often needing half a day to finish a task that any of his brothers could complete in an hour. Fergal decided it would have to be Fish.

His heart raced when his father told him. His mother placed her hand on his shoulder; he wasn't sure whether to cry or cheer. For the next few days, as he prepared to leave, his emotions rose and fell like the ocean waves he'd soon come to love. He'd miss his brothers and sisters, his gruff, hard father and practical mother, his swims in the lake. But the prospect of actually helping his family made him feel a good six inches taller.

On the day he left, the good-byes were short and consisted mostly of affectionate punches and brief hugs. Conor's punch was not entirely affectionate; he left a painful memento on Fish's shoulder in the form of a purple and blue bruise. His mother held him in her arms longer than she ever had before and his sister Roisin, who could carve just about anything from a hunk of wood, handed him a newly whittled fish. He could just close his fist around it. "For my brother the swimmer," she said. Then she whispered, "Who is going to help me survive under Queen Mary's rule?"

"And who will warn me of worms and muddied milk?" he asked.

"I hope you won't have to worry about either."

For the better part of two days, Fish walked with his father along a puddle-filled road traveled by men on horseback and the occasional carriage. They lodged one night in a large stable, taunted by the sights, sounds, and smells of healthy horses, reminding them of poor Shamrock. They arrived in the city early in the afternoon, and the new world was both exciting and frightening. Fish had never seen more than three buildings in one place, but here there were hundreds, all stacked together and standing three times as tall as the cottage on the farm. Yet the color had been drained from everything; the familiar green fields and trees were gone, replaced with varying shades of brown. The entire city looked like it needed a bath.

Smoke billowed from chimneys and doorways and burned his nostrils. The heavenly scents of freshly baked breads and roasted meats mingled evenly with the foul stench of outhouses and trash-filled alleys. One moment he wanted to savor the air, the next he felt like wrapping a cloth around his mouth and nose to block it out.

He stayed close to his father as they walked through the dry and dusty streets. They met his father's brother Gerry in a public house called the Burren. The place was dark and miserable, a wooden cave that blocked out all sunlight, and they sat in a tight booth near the door. Uncle Gerry, a large man with large hands who, like Fergal, was prone to grunting, ordered two ales for himself and his brother. Fish was next to his father, pressed between him and the wall.

Strange people filled the place: women with bright purple makeup on their faces and round, ugly men with blotchy red skin. But his father was uninterested in the scene. He and Uncle Gerry grunted and grumbled back and forth. It sounded like they each had food stuck in their throats, but Fish eventually realized that they were, in their own way, conducting a very real conversation.

Finally, Fish heard his father say, "So it's decided, then."

He turned to his father. What was decided?

"Frgggghhhh," Uncle Gerry responded.

"Gruffff," his father answered back.

Fergal stepped out of the booth. Fish slid toward the end, ready to follow, but Uncle Gerry reached across and placed one of his large hands on his shoulder, stopping him. Fish looked up at his father.

"You'll stay here now."

Fergal picked up his glass from the wooden table and

drank the last of the brown ale inside. He placed his hand on Fish's head. "Be careful," he said.

The first few weeks were difficult. Fish missed his brothers and sisters, those rare moments around the table when nobody was fighting and everyone was full of food and cheer. But he did not miss digging into the soil, cleaning the filthy pigpens, or having to deal with the farm's ornery, stubborn sheep. The city — a chaotic mass of people small and large, of sailors and merchants speaking French, Portuguese, and Italian — kept his mind away from home. Winding streets and narrow alleyways fed off wide thoroughfares lined with people selling vegetables, wool, and various trinkets out of wooden carts. Women wore bright dresses and large hats, and the men swilled from bottles in the middle of the day. The city, in a way, was like a book. No, it didn't have pages and paragraphs, but it was filled with life and variety, sounds and smells. The city was a living, breathing, endlessly interesting book.

There were young people, too, like him, but he never saw them playing or having fun. They were running errands, working in the inns and offices, selling baubles, and they rarely offered him more than a nod. As for his own work, well, Fish didn't exactly understand what sort of business his uncle Gerry conducted. All he knew was that he was charged with running packages of various shapes and sizes from one part of the city to another, and that his uncle had enough clients to keep him moving from morning until night, when Fish would collapse, exhausted, onto his bed.

Despite his fatigue, Fish never complained. He worked ever harder and faster, straight through the rest of fall, winter, and spring. He asked Uncle Gerry when he might have a break, even just for two days, so he could visit the farm, but his uncle only grunted a few times before responding, "Soon, soon, but I can't afford to lose you now." Fish wrote several times, and sent money on a regular basis, but he rarely heard back, and the few replies were short. Uncle Gerry would see the brief notes and grunt, "My brother's not much with a pen."

Often Fish wondered if anyone at home actually missed him. And he had so many questions, too. Had the girls gotten much bigger? Were his brothers fighting more now that he was gone? Had Roisin led a revolution against the domineering Queen Mary? He kept the fish she gave him in his pocket and rubbed it when he longed for his family, as if this action might magically bring him home.

But he was too busy to wonder for long. Fish ran letters to the crowded and frightful prison, delivered packages to the brewery, and whisked notes from the grand houses on the city's edges to boats down at the docks. These last jobs were his favorites, for they brought him near the water. He loved to race down, close his eyes, and breathe in the sea air. He'd get close to the boats, inspect their hulls, decks, and sails for signs of distant adventures. He thought he could smell hints of the open ocean stuck to their sails.

Therefore, it was entirely understandable that Fish smiled so brightly that summer morning when Uncle Gerry handed him a leather purse and informed him that he was to take it to the docks. Yet Fish's smile did not please his uncle.

Uncle Gerry glared, one hand still holding the top of the purse. "This is important."

"Yes, of course."

"No," Uncle Gerry said, pausing. "This is *very* important."

"I understand," Fish said.

"You will deliver this to the *Mary*, a passenger ship docked in the harbor, bound for America. You will deliver it, specifically, to a certain Reginald Swift, who will be sailing on that ship."

"Yes."

"He is an uncommonly small man with uncommonly large eyeglasses. Aged about thirty years, a good few less than your father and myself. He is expecting you."

Fish waited with one hand on the bottom of the purse while Uncle Gerry still gripped the top. He'd done hundreds of deliveries already. This sounded no more challenging than the rest. Why, then, was his uncle so concerned?

Uncle Gerry grunted, glowered, grunted again, then pulled his hand away. The purse itself was altogether unimpressive, yet it felt like it was filled with coins. "Are these —"

"The contents are not your concern." Fish turned to leave, but his uncle stopped him. "Fish?"

"Yes?" he asked.

"I realize that I stress the importance of all your assignments, but this one is especially critical. These particular clients . . . they do not tolerate mistakes. You must not fail."

Fish replied with a solemn nod, then sped out the door, down the street, and through the alleys he'd come to know so well. Within minutes, Fish had reached the harbor and found the *Mary*, which was twice as large as any other ship tied to the docks, and twice as grand, too. Sailors and dockworkers were rolling aboard huge wooden barrels filled with water, beer, salted pork and beef, biscuits and butter. He'd heard that these ships could carry as many as two hundred people for a journey that lasted more than a month.

Some of the passengers were out on the broad deck, others standing below on the overcrowded dock. What had Uncle Gerry said? Uncommonly small, with uncommonly large eyeglasses. Fish wondered just how small someone had to be to qualify as uncommonly so. Walking onto the dock, he studied the faces and stopped as a short, bald man stepped toward him. No, that wouldn't be Reginald Swift. He was only a little shorter than Fish and he didn't have glasses, either.

A quartet of ladies in very large yellow dresses briefly blocked his way, but Fish squeezed between them and spotted a man leaning against one of the pier's tall, worn wooden columns. It had to be him. Short? Very much so. A sailor walked in front of Swift, and he looked like a child next to the man. The glasses, too, matched Uncle Gerry's description. Big and black-rimmed, they took up nearly half his face.

And these glasses were effective, for Reginald Swift obviously spotted the purse from a distance: His eyes widened. A wave of relief washed through Fish. Uncle Gerry had entrusted him with an important task and he was about to complete it successfully. Perhaps Uncle Gerry would even tell his father. Fish imagined his father clapping him proudly on the back, the way he'd congratulate Patrick, Michael, and Conor after a hard day's work in the —

Fish crashed to the ground, his shoulder driven hard into the wooden dock. He blinked, breathed, felt the purse in his fingers. What had happened? Was that Swift hurrying his way? Before he could determine for certain, someone knocked the diminutive man to the dock.

Fish tried to sit up, but someone yanked him up to his feet by his collar before he had the chance. Still confused, he found himself standing eye to eye with a boy about his age.

"Release the purse, and I will release you," the boy snarled.

This boy was strong — even stronger than his brothers — but Fish wasn't about to hand over that purse. He would not fail his uncle Gerry. Not after all the hard work he'd done in the last few months.

He gripped the purse tighter and tried to pull away, but the boy struck him in the jaw with the back of his free hand. Pain shot through his head. Holding tight to the purse as the boy tried to yank it away, Fish cried, "Can't we . . . discuss this . . . in a more civilized way?"

The boy drove his fist into Fish's stomach. He crumpled

to the dock, his arms wrapped around his midsection. Apparently the answer was no.

The purse! Placing a fist on the ground, Fish steadied himself and stood up. He saw the boy hurrying away through the crowd.

Ignoring the sickening pain in his stomach, Fish ran after him and leaped at the boy's legs. They wrestled toward the edge of the dock, and then the boy smiled, saying: "Goodbye, pest!" He pushed Fish over the side, sending him splashing down into the cool water below.

Immediately Fish pulled back to the surface. Treading water, he scoured the docks. The boy was out of sight. No one seemed to have noticed the theft; passengers, sailors, and dockworkers were carrying on as before.

A thick rope splashed down in front of him. Reginald Swift was up on the dock, urging him to hurry. He looked frightened. Fish pulled himself out of the water. "The boy and another man . . . they went that way!" he said, his eyes wild as he pointed down the dock. "And if you don't catch them, my mother will be furious!"

"Your mother?" Fish asked. Why was this grown man talking about his mother?

"Just hurry! If you lose that purse, it could mean both our lives!"

Fish studied the crowd in both directions. There! The boy, and another man with him. He could see them turning down a dock a few hundred feet away. Dripping wet, his stomach and neck now dull to the pain, Fish sprinted ahead to the dock. Not a single boat was tied up, yet he was certain he'd seen them turn this way. A man who looked like a farmer was leaning against a pylon, smoking a pipe. Behind him, three sailors were standing against the wall outside an alehouse, their faces turned up to the sun. A thin, bald, wrinkled gentleman in official dress walked quickly by, passing a mother and her young children. But that ruffian boy and his friend were nowhere in sight.

His heart was pounding. Failure. Reginald Swift said their lives were at stake, but all Fish could think about was the terrible prospect of disappointing Uncle Gerry and his father and mother. And what would his brothers say?

He had no choice but to find the thieves before they slipped away for good. He was about to run back in the other direction and scour the town square when he saw two heads, then a rowboat moving swiftly away from the dock. They were heading toward the far side of the harbor. There, anchored near the shore, floated a thoroughly menacing boat.

SNEAKING UP ON SCALAWAGS

Fish stripped off his shirt, kicked off his shoes — which were, incidentally, the last pair of shoes he would ever wear — and leaped headfirst into the cool harbor.

The rowboat was too far ahead and moving too quickly. There was no way he could catch them before they reached the ship, so he swam slowly and quietly with his head barely above the water, hoping they wouldn't hear or see him. If he could somehow climb up onto the boat and find the purse, then he could simply slip back down into the water and swim for shore without anyone noticing.

Fish had learned a fact or two about boats since he'd been working in the city. This craft, from the size and shape of it, and the way its single mast leaned toward the back, was a sloop. One of the dockworkers had told him they were fast, easy to handle, capable of holding fifty men or more. The man had also said they were favored by a certain class of seafaring men known as pirates, but Fish pushed this notion to the back of his mind. Not every sloop was crewed by pirates. The boy and his partner were probably stowaways. Thieves who rowed ashore to prey upon people like him.

Still, he would have to be quiet. Just to be safe. He watched the rowboat pull up alongside the sloop and swam away from it, toward the front, so he wouldn't be seen. A long, thick, slimy cable ran down from the boat to the floor of the harbor, where an anchor held it fast. He could climb that to reach the deck. But first Fish stopped and stared up at the sloop. Normally, oceangoing craft had a wooden statue of some sort at the bow, a beautiful maiden or mermaid. But the carving here resembled a monster: charred, cut, and slashed in places, all of its paint chipped or worn. One of the arms looked like it had been sawed off at the elbow.

Fish had heard that the point of these statues was to win the ocean's favor by presenting her with a beautiful figure. In that effort, this boat had surely failed.

No one stood watch above that half-burned mermaid. If he moved fast, he could reach the deck undetected. He hung upside down from the slippery cable and climbed upward using his hands and feet. His hands soon became tired, his arms and shoulders, too, but he kept scurrying. Mr. Swift would undoubtedly send word of his failure to Uncle Gerry if he didn't mend the situation soon. With this in mind, Fish climbed faster, grabbed the wooden railing at the bow, jumped over, and crouched at the front of the boat.

The deck was wildly busy, so no one noticed him. This was a good thing, too, since these men were clearly not regular merchants or sailors. There were no uniforms among them; their clothes were mostly ragged and worn, patched together in several places, as if each shirt had been sewn together from the remains of five or six others. They were darker, more wind-whipped than normal sailors, and smelled as if they bathed in river mud, ate from a pig's trough, and kept rotting eggs in their pockets. These men were pirates.

Fish had heard about pirates. Stories of these seagoing marauders even reached the farm on occasion, and they were often talked about in the city, where many people departing for the long sail to America hoped and prayed aloud that they wouldn't be raided along the way.

Yet this was no time to be frightened. He had to push forward.

A large section of a folded-up sail was lying flat on the deck beside him. Fish grabbed the thick canvas, hoping to dry his face and hands.

"Release that, boy!" a man yelled. "Can you not see that I am at work?"

Thin and well dressed, more like a gentleman than a pirate, the man was hunched over the far end of the sailcloth, busily working with a needle and thread. He was entirely bald, with a bright red face, small eyes, and hollow cheeks that suggested he didn't eat well. His clothes were nothing like those of his shipmates — the cuffs and collar of his shirt looked to be made from the finest fabrics, with gilded buttons that shined in the sunlight. He swigged from a bottle of wine, then waved Fish away without looking at him, as if he were a dog begging for scraps of food.

The other men were similarly preoccupied. A few were scrubbing the deck, others were stowing heavy oak barrels down below, still more were repairing patches of wood and sharpening long, gleaming blades on rough gray stones. They were all toiling except for a small group of men standing before the lone cabin, at the far end of the boat.

The thief was with them, arms crossed on his chest. His pose reminded Fish of the way Patrick would stand when he was talking to their parents, trying to act older. He'd press his shoulders back, keep his chin high, and scrunch his forehead as if it were a gargantuan task to keep all the large and important thoughts in his head from rushing out at once. This boy, too, was trying to appear wise beyond his years.

Fish had to get back there quickly, without being stopped, and to do that he had to look like he belonged. A large, worn brush with a long handle leaned against a nearby railing; he grabbed it and walked with his head down toward the back.

Stopping short of the group, Fish got down on one knee and pretended to scrub the deck. There were four of them. He looked closely at the thief from the dock. He had lightly freckled skin, much like Michael, though it was also tinted brown from the sun. His hair was straight, short, and dark brown, and he had the muscles of a young man, not a boy.

One of the men — the leader, he guessed — looked to be about his father's age. He was distinguished, with tightly curled gray hair, fine clothes, and the stem of an unlit pipe held between his lips. His ears were large, pressed back flat against his head, and his skin was tanned, with a faded but thick red scar on his chin. A thin, pronounced nose added to the air of nobility.

The man on his right, the shortest among them, was more

vile than noble. He had long black hair, a ragged beard, and dark eyes hiding beneath bushy, unkempt eyebrows. Dull silver hoops were stuck through his lower lip and ears. He was tremendously thick, as if he'd been hit on the head with a massive hammer and compacted into that short frame, and he bore evidence of a great many wounds. Old scars slashed across his forehead, both cheeks, and his chin.

The fourth pirate was an absolute giant. He was a human oak tree, a head taller than Fish's father and three times as wide. His large nose, bent in the middle, leaned to one side near the tip. His beard was deep, dark brown, and thick. It looked rough enough to sand the wooden deck smooth, and he scratched it with fingers as large as sausages.

The giant and the boy were quiet; the other two were arguing.

The short, thick, scarred man grabbed the purse. "Treachery! That's what I call this, Cobb."

"Captain Cobb," the other man stressed.

"You won't be captain for long if you betray your crew. Not even your giant friend here could calm fifty angry, armed men."

"I have not betrayed my crew, Scab."

"Scar" would have been a better name, Fish thought.

"I might not have been educated at Cambridge, but I am no fool." He held out the purse. "Do you mean to tell me that you sent this boy ashore simply to steal a bag of coins? Can you honestly say that this has nothing to do with your beloved chain? Can you assure the men that you do not plan to enlist us in yet another fruitless quest for that mythical string of jewels? Tell me, Nate," he said, turning to the boy, "would you rather cross the ocean in search of something that might not exist? Or would you follow the course of a right-minded pirate and patrol the shipping and transit lanes for frigates and galleons loaded with goods and riches?"

Fish watched the boy, Nate, hesitate. He was being asked to choose a side, either with Cobb or the one they called Scab, and didn't know how to respond. He mumbled, "I . . ."

"Nathaniel," Cobb said, "you do not have to answer that."

"No, but you should answer, Cobb. Unless these coins truly bear no relation to your mythical chain." Scab waited for a reply, then resumed. "In that case, I will deliver this purse to Foot, who will, in accordance with custom, divide the sum amongst the crew."

"No!"

All four turned toward Fish. Had he actually shouted that aloud? He looked back down at the deck. Perhaps they would ignore him if he resumed scrubbing.

The sharp edge of a blade, held under his chin, convinced him otherwise.

"Up," Scab said.

"That's the courier," said the boy, Nathaniel. "The one who was carrying the purse."

"And you are here to retrieve your package?" Cobb asked.

Fish couldn't think, let alone respond, with that piece of metal below his chin.

"Scab," Cobb said, "lower your blade."

Fish thrust back his shoulders and tried to stand taller. He felt flimsy, standing there wearing only a pair of very wet pants, but he had been wronged. He coughed and deepened his voice. "Yes. I am here to retrieve it."

"This was stolen from you?" Scab asked. "How terrible! An absolute scandal in a perfectly reputable city such as this. Here," he said, handing over the purse, "take it back. It's yours."

Fish gripped it with both hands. It couldn't be that easy. This act had to be part of Scab's argument with Cobb.

Nate tried to grab the purse back, but Scab knocked away his hand. The boy then reached for his cutlass, inciting Scab to do the same, but the giant stepped between them before their blades could clash.

Fish had the purse. And the railing was only a few steps away. He could dive off and start swimming. He might reach the shore before they caught him in that rowboat. What other choice did he have? He had no intention of fighting his way off the boat, and these men did not appear to be the type one could reason with.

Now was the time. Fish took a deep breath, sprang up onto the railing, and dove off the side of the boat.

Reluctant Recruit

Fish needed to swim fast, to get away before they had time to catch him in the rowboat. The shore wasn't far, so if he swam hard he could get there quickly.

But he needed both hands. He ducked under the water, took one end of the rope that he used as a belt, tied it around the purse, then resurfaced and began to swim.

There was a loud splash in the water behind him. He stopped and looked back at the boat. The men were all at the railing, yelling and pointing.

Somebody was in the water, but he wasn't making any progress. Was it Nate, the boy who had stolen the purse in the first place? No. The man in the water was bearded, his face home to numerous silver hoops. It was Scab. He was flailing, waving his arms. He was drowning. Bubbles popped at the surface; the pirate had gone under. Yet no one was diving in to save him. If Fish raced for shore, Scab might die. And he could not let that happen.

He kicked back toward the boat. Fish breathed in deep and dove. The water was dark and slightly murky, but he found him quickly; Scab had sunk like a rock. Fish grabbed him by the shirt and kicked with all his might toward the surface.

Seconds later they emerged, the pirate limp and lifeless. A

few of the men on deck cheered as Fish, his arm wrapped across Scab's chest, swam to the anchor cable. He grabbed hold, then pulled Scab's hands toward it, too.

Once the pirate felt the thick cable, he slowly came back to life. He was dazed, but alive. Fish was relieved; for a moment he thought he had arrived too late. He closed his eyes and breathed in deeply. He had saved one of their men. They would be obliged to let him return to shore with Mr. Swift's purse.

Or not.

Cold, wet metal pressed against his neck. The smell of the pirate's sharp, stinking breath filled his nostrils, carrying undercurrents of old onions and hints of something even more potent. Was it rotting, unwashed feet?

The pirate flashed a crooked, false, spine-shivering smile. His teeth were brown and broken. "Give me the purse."

"But I saved you."

"A poor decision on your part," Scab replied, pushing the blade in slightly harder.

There was no choice. Fish untied the purse and handed it to the ungrateful beast. Scab bit down on the top of the purse with his brown, cracked teeth and scurried up the cable. Watching the pirate climb, Fish considered letting go and swimming away. He could be rid of this boat and its untrustworthy, ungrateful crew for good.

No. He would not leave without that purse. He followed Scab back up to the boat.

On deck, Scab was shouting at Cobb, who stood resolutely outside his cabin. "The men deserve a prize, not a dream, Cobb!" he yelled. "They deserve a prize!"

The giant, who hadn't said a word since Fish had been on board, wrapped his massive fingers around Fish's shoulders. Those fingers could have cracked his bones as easily as eggshells, so he did not resist. As Scab continued his curse-filled rant, the giant led Fish toward the rear of the boat.

Half naked, Fish shivered under the gray sky. Cobb motioned to the giant, who stepped into the cabin, reemerged with a shirt, and tossed it to Fish. It was several sizes too large, but he pulled it on hastily, sat, and brought his knees to his chest.

Two men, including the bald, red-faced, fancily dressed man who had been repairing the sails, were dragging Scab down below, attempting to soothe his temper. But Scab continued yelling and shouting about "raiding" and "taking a prize instead of hunting down a myth."

Fish studied the captain. Cobb seemed to be swayed in some way, or oddly sympathetic, as though he were truly considering Scab's opinion. His voice slightly shaky from the cold, Fish asked, "Why is he so angry?"

"In part, I suppose, because I had my very large friend Moravius here throw him overboard. He gave you that purse, so I felt it was his responsibility to retrieve it once you jumped."

"But he didn't know how to swim —"

"That is not my concern," Cobb shot back. "Furthermore, Scab and I have a theoretical disagreement regarding the proper way to operate as a paperless privateer —"

"You mean 'pirate,' right?" Fish asked.

"No," Cobb replied, "I do not. When we are within range of the home ports of the Royal Navy, we are paperless privateers. On the other side of the ocean, where the skies are bright and the waters clear, we are pirates."

Fish stood up. His condition was improving. He stopped shivering. The shirt stifled the chill, and this conversation was far more civilized than all the screaming and fighting. "So, this theoretical disagreement —"

"No more questions!" Cobb snapped. "Right now the only question is what we are going to do with you."

The captain studied him for a moment, then watched his crew busily working on deck. They were pulling up anchor, hoisting sails, shouting orders from one side of the ship to the other. The sloop, Fish realized, was leaving the harbor. This was not an encouraging development.

Fish eyed the purse. There was a very simple answer to Cobb's question. "You can return my property and allow me to be on my way."

"Your property?" Cobb laughed. He tossed the purse from one hand to the other. "Your property? There is no rightful owner to the contents of this purse. It belongs to whoever is intelligent or resourceful enough to have it in their possession. Thus, at present, it is very much ours," he said, and then tossed it to the giant, Moravius. "Take that into my cabin."

The giant walked off without a word. Why didn't he speak? He understood basic orders, so he wasn't entirely simple. Perhaps he was a mute.

"I do admire your perseverance, though," Cobb said. "You handle yourself well in the water. As you saw, none of the men dove in to save Scab. Some would have him drown, yet he has his allies, too. But they could not save him because they cannot swim. This skill is all too rare, I'm afraid." He briefly pulled down on the end of his long nose, as if he were attempting to lengthen it further. "What is your name?"

He started to say "Maurice," then corrected himself. "Fish."

"Yes, of course! How fitting. Normally a new member of my crew doesn't receive a name of that sort until he distinguishes himself in some significant manner, but since you have arrived with a perfectly suitable one intact, we will make an exception."

The captain's eyebrows angled down, as though he was suddenly deep in thought, and he began studying Fish with a familiar concentration. His uncle Gerry bore the same look when attempting to estimate the value of a piece of jewelry.

"A proficiency in swimming. An unyielding commitment to assigned tasks. Some intriguing qualities for a pirate, but you are physically untested," he said, reaching down and grabbing Fish's hands. "Small. They don't look like they have seen a day of hard work."

Fish yanked his hands away. What an insult! And a completely inaccurate one. No, he didn't spend half the day with his hands deep in the dirt or yanking on ropes aboard a sailing ship, but he worked as hard as anyone. This man, who had known him for all of a few minutes, had no right to say otherwise. "I resent —"

Cobb cut him off. "We do need another boy aboard. Someone to swab the decks, clean the seats of easement, assist the gunners . . . given your talent for swimming, I suppose you could scrape the hull when we are at anchor. A barnacle-free boat makes for far smoother sailing, you know."

Fish did not know, but he could tell that this was irrelevant. Cobb was talking as much to himself as he was to Fish. The captain took his pipe and jabbed the mouthpiece into the air. "Yes. It is decided. You will join the crew."

As Cobb issued his ruling, one of the sails snapped full with wind, and the boat began edging forward.

Jump. That was his first thought. Simply jump off the boat, without the purse, and swim straight for the shore. Yet Fish did not move.

The captain called over a dark-skinned boy who'd been scrubbing the deck nearby. "Daniel, show our new crewmate here how to freshen up this wood."

And with that, Cobb was finished with him. He strode back toward his cabin. Daniel stopped to study the newest member of the crew, so Fish returned his stare. The boy had very short black hair, tightly curled, a flat, wide nose, and large, bright eyes. He was about Fish's age and height, but his shoulders were as broad as those of a grown man, and he had the scarred, weathered hands of someone much older, too. He had not enjoyed a gentle life.

To this boy, Fish must have looked like a fool. His shirt was so big and billowy it could have passed for a dress.

Daniel handed him a brush with a long wooden handle. "Welcome to the *Scurvy Mistress*," he said. "This is a swab, and you will soon think of it as a third arm."

"Excuse me?" he said. "The what?"

"The *Scurvy Mistress*. That's her name."

"Her?"

"The boat!"

"Oh, right." He should have known that. He did know that; he had heard sailors talk about their boats this way in the past. They all referred to them as if they were women.

"You've never sailed before?"

"No, I . . ."

Throwing his arm around Fish's shoulder, Daniel pointed to the front of the boat, then the back, right, and left. In turn, he said, "Bow. Stern. Starboard. Larboard. Got that?"

Fish nodded.

"Good. Remember that, and stay out of everyone's way, and you should survive." Daniel pointed at the swab. "You have to work, though, if you're going to be part of this crew."

"I'm not a part of the crew."

"If you are on this boat, you are either part of the crew or a prisoner, and you do not want to be a prisoner. So do what I do, or else one of these ugly gentlemen will slam the butt of a pistol into the back of your head. Which is, I assure you, not a particularly enjoyable experience."

Fish needed no further convincing. He mimicked Daniel and pressed the swab to the slimy wooden surface, scrubbing forward and back.

"Not bad," Daniel said, watching him. "Now, what do you mean about not being part of this crew?"

"I'm only here because that thief Nate —"

Daniel laughed. "Nate the Great."

"What?"

"I call him that because he thinks he is going to be some sort of great pirate captain one day."

"Right, well, he stole something that I was asked to deliver, so I followed him here to get it back because if I don't deliver it, Uncle Gerry will never let me work for him again, and then I won't be able to send any money back home and my family . . . my family will . . ."

Fish thought of the carving Roisin had given him; did he still have it? He shoved his hands into his pockets. Thankfully, the wooden fish was there. He gripped it tight, as if it might give him strength.

"Are you concerned about money?" Daniel asked.

No, he was not. Or perhaps that wasn't true. Fish hadn't thought about it before, but in a way, money was at the root of it all. If money were of no concern, Shamrock's death would not have been so dire, and he never would have been sent to the city in the first place. "Yes," he said finally. "I suppose I am concerned about money."

Daniel resumed scrubbing, motioned for Fish to do the same. "Then this is the position you want. Not city work. What is it that you do now?"

"I'm a messenger."

"Ha! Earning little more than a mat and a meal, no doubt. Now, that's fine for most people our age, but not me. I've been on boats my entire life. And I've been privateering, or," he added in a whisper, "pirating, since I was seven. This crew is the best I've sailed with. Captain Cobb is probably the smartest man on the sea, and Scab is one of the toughest, with a feel for the winds and the waves like no one I have ever seen. Thimble" — he pointed toward the red-faced, skeletal man who'd been mending the sails — "doesn't really love anything but his clothes and his wine. The man drinks all day and would rather have an enemy slice open his own skin than one of his precious shirts, but he can patch anything with a bit of thread. Sails, jackets, pants, even men."

"Men?" Fish asked.

"Sure. He's also our surgeon. Sews you up if you've been shot or stabbed." Daniel pointed to a sailor with a head the size of a melon and a belly large enough to fit a cow. "Sammy the Stomach has the appetite of ten men, but more importantly, he's probably one of the best gunners on the ocean. He could knock a spyglass out of an opposing captain's hands with a cannonball. That said, most of the time we don't even need to fire a shot. Once the other crews get a glimpse of Moravius, they run the white flag. He could scare a tidal wave, that man. Now, you put all these rovers together on a single ship and you know what this adds up to?"

A group that would give the devil nightmares, Fish thought.

"Gold. I already have more money than my parents ever dreamed of. In four or five years, I should have enough gold to retire and buy myself a big house. A house full of friends and food. Yes," he continued, "if it's money you need, forget about working in the city. You need to be out on the seas."

Daniel stopped scrubbing. Someone was yelling and all the men were putting aside their tools and tasks, walking toward the two boys. Fish took a few steps back, but Daniel laughed and placed one of his weathered hands on his shoulder. "They're not coming for us." He pointed behind him; Cobb and Moravius were standing there, in front of the cabin. "See that?" he asked, pointing to a black flag making its way up the mast. "That means it's time for action."

The flag flapped open in the wind, revealing the image of a white hourglass. Fish must have looked puzzled because Daniel answered his question before he even asked.

"I know, where's the old skull and crossbones? Captain Cobb prefers the hourglass because it reminds us that our time here is limited and that we've got to make the most of it while we can."

Cobb coughed twice, then faced the mass of men. Scab, black eyes narrowed beneath his dense eyebrows, had stepped up from below.

"Scab, your first mate, has convinced me that the time has come for us to take a prize," Cobb announced.

Many in the crowd cheered and stomped their feet. Fish could feel the deck shake. Cobb and Scab glared at each other, as if this were just a new, more subtle phase of their argument. But the hint of a smile — an ugly, unnatural one, but still a smile — was clear on Scab's scarred face.

"Although I imagine we might agree that it would be wise to avoid taking a prize in these waters," Cobb continued, "I believe that this target is too promising to ignore."

Many of the men yelled excitedly, yet Fish was surprised to see that a number of others hardly reacted at all; they looked disinterested. A group of older men, each of whom was wearing an eye patch, actually appeared to be disappointed.

"At noon tomorrow we will take the *Mary*, a freighter bound for America. Her passengers, and one in particular, carry with them tremendous riches. And I'm sure that the *Mary* herself would be grateful if we were to relieve her of all that extra weight, allowing her a smoother, swifter sail across the sea."

Another cheer followed, and then the crew refocused its efforts to prepare the ship. Daniel tossed aside his brush; he was obviously not pleased with the news.

"What does he mean when he says you're going to 'take' her?" Fish asked.

The boy was solemn when he answered. "He means we're going to launch a raid."

No Grime Too Green

Fish spent the remainder of the day brushing the deck free of grime and slime. On several occasions he became so focused on his appointed task that he forgot entirely he was on a pirate ship, cleaning decks for some of the most dangerous and dirtiest men on the seas. Once, after successfully removing a particularly stubborn stain, he actually smiled.

There was a call for supper near the end of the day, but not even the powerful hunger roaring in his stomach convinced him to venture down into the depths of that ship, where all he heard was shouting and yelling and a not particularly joyous form of singing. Thankfully, Daniel was kind enough to bring him a mug of water and a few rolls. They were hard as rocks and settled in his stomach like stones, but they were enough, and he tucked himself under some sailcloth near the bow and let the boat rock him into a deep sleep.

At dawn he arose to the familiar sound of a cock crowing. He hadn't heard that sound since he'd left home, but his rough canvas blanket, the cool, wet wind, and the swaying of the boat reminded him that he was far from the farm. He sat up, yawned, looked toward the back of the boat — the stern, that's what Daniel said — and saw the giant, Moravius, standing with his hands cupped to his mouth, crowing.

Very well, that settled one question. Moravius was most certainly not mute.

"An odd way to wake us all," Daniel said from behind him, "but it does work."

"He crows?" Fish said.

"Don't ask him why. He won't answer. So, how did you sleep?"

Fish yawned in reply.

"Not well, I see. I woke up early myself, thought I'd come up here to see if you'd jumped off during the night."

Before Fish could answer, the handle of a swab smacked him in the chest. The stink of rotting onions and feet replaced the delightfully fresh air; though he'd only met him the day before, Fish could already recognize Scab with his eyes closed. The pirate coughed and spat something black and thick onto the deck, then pointed to the vile glob.

"You were supposed to have this scrubbed yesterday," Scab barked. "Get back to work, you lazy cur!"

Without a word, Fish took the brush and did as he was ordered. And he planned to continue doing so for the remainder of the morning. He would follow their orders and live according to their strange rules until the raid began. Then he would follow his own directives: He would launch a raid of his own.

The key to his plan was the fact that Reginald Swift was scheduled to sail on the *Mary*, the very same boat they now planned to attack. This meant that Fish still had a chance to complete his delivery. Yes, he'd have to retrieve the coins first, then find Swift aboard the other boat. It would not be easy. But it was the only chance he had. And this time, he would not fail.

The *Scurvy Mistress* was heading southwest along the coast, carried along by a gentle but steady breeze. They were passing a stretch of the country his mother once said was more beautiful than heaven itself. Bright green hills sat atop ragged, sandy cliffs. The blue-green ocean stretched out before them under a canopy of clear blue sky. Yet the view did not last, as fog and mist began blowing in from the horizon.

The call for breakfast came and went. Fish was still too frightened to venture below. Daniel saved him from starving once more, bringing him another few rock-hard rolls, a cold, salty, tough piece of meat, and a mug of grayish, strange-tasting milk.

Late that morning the *Scurvy Mistress* turned around a point and lingered, without anchoring, in a deep, sheltered cove. The air was now thick with mist, the sun a bright smear of white high in the sky.

The plan, Daniel told him, was to wait there until the *Mary* came within view — they had purposely not advanced too far during the night — and then pursue her. The *Scurvy Mistress* would have no difficulty overtaking the heavy frigate, Fish heard the men say. She was made for speed, the other ship designed to carry cargo. And in light or little wind, she also had the advantage of oars. Sixteen men in the very belly of the boat, each handling great wooden oars that reached out and down into the water through small holes in the hull, could power the *Scurvy Mistress* up to a perfectly respectable speed. Outmaneuvering the lumbering *Mary* would be easy.

The men had been busy when they first set sail, but now, with the raid imminent, they were frenzied. Anything that wasn't part of the deck, or bolted to it, was sent down below. Large pieces of cloth and canvas were hung over the railings. A group of pirates sat near the bow, each one bent over his own pair of pistols, polishing, inspecting, and loading them.

Nathaniel, the thief, hurried past him, then stopped and turned, clearly surprised to see Fish. "You're part of our crew now?"

"I am," he said in a stern tone. "The name is Fish."

"And you fight like one, too," Nate quipped. Then he stifled the smile. "Sorry. That was too easy. And this is good. We could use more boys. With you there will be three of us — yourself, Daniel, and I — and we have to stay together."

Fish nodded. "Of course."

Nate looked around to see if anyone was listening, then lowered his voice and leaned in. "Speaking of which, would you mind telling me . . . nothing. Forget about it."

"What is it?" Fish pressed.

"Well," Nate said, "when I came after you on the docks, was I intimidating? You know, like a real pirate?"

Fish wasn't sure how to respond. "I suppose. . . ."

"A touch frightening, perhaps?"

The boy was looking at him eagerly. Yet there was nothing particularly intimidating about him now, nor the day before. He had wrapped a rag around the top of his head and smeared some sort of black gunk beneath his eyes. And yes, he was strong. But he was strong for a boy, not for a man. A beard, or even the beginnings of one, might have enhanced his fearsomeness, but his freckled face had yet to see any significant hair growth. His blue eyes were fitting for a sailor — they matched the color of a clear sky near dusk — but for a pirate, a darker shade would have been more forbidding.

Yet Nate did not need to know any of this. There would be no harm in telling him what he wanted to hear. "Yes," Fish said after a moment. "Terribly frightening."

"Thanks!" he answered. "Godspeed with the raid today. Remember to keep your cutlass out and your eyes and ears open!"

Nate was off before Fish had a chance to point out that he had no cutlass. The closest thing he had to a weapon was the swab.

Although Captain Cobb oversaw the activity from the upper deck at the stern, Scab was obviously in charge of the details. As he walked among the men, he clapped them on their shoulders and backs, handing out pieces of red cloth, which they tied around their arms and heads. He came to Fish, stopped, then laughed and walked on.

Fish called to Daniel, who was securing the ties on one of the sails nearby. "Why the red?"

"We wear them so you know who is on the other side. It can be hard to see with the smoke. Here," he said, pulling an extra red rag from his pocket, "wrap this around your head to be safe."

As Fish tied the rag around his forehead, he turned and saw Nate approaching Scab. "I want to be one of the boarders," Nate said.

"A boarder? Are you ready for that?"

"Yes, sir," Nate answered. "I'm a good shot, sir, with a quick blade."

In a blur Scab unsheathed his cutlass and swung at Nate. The boy responded just as quickly, removing his own blade and blocking Scab's strike.

Fish tensed, but this was no fight. This was a test.

"True enough," Scab said. He lowered his blade. "You may join the boarding party. And if you survive, I will consider you for a permanent position."

Nate smiled, then hurried off toward the bow, where he joined the men who were preparing their pistols. Still working on the sails, Daniel scoffed. "He's too young to be a boarder. I doubt he'll make it back."

Fish was going to ask just what it meant to be a boarder when he heard a call from high up the mast. All the men turned and stared to the south. The mostly hidden sun was high in the sky, so it had to be close to noon, yet the fog was still thick enough to obscure the horizon. There, from within the mist, a massive ship was emerging.

Scab shouted, "OARS!"

A few seconds later the boat began lurching forward. Fish ran to the starboard side. Below, eight oars were splashing and stroking in unison.

"That's the job you do not want," Daniel told him. "Trapped in the belly of the boat, your feet sitting in brackish water, pulling on those oars for hours at a time when the wind has gone to sleep."

"SAILS!" Scab shouted next, and the *Scurvy Mistress* began to accelerate.

Before long, the *Mary* was only a short swim away. Fish was going to ask Daniel how they'd proceed when he heard Cobb yell. It sounded like he shouted "stomach," but he wasn't sure. The next word, though, was clear:

"FIRE!"

A deck-shaking explosion followed seconds later. A cannon shot sped through the air toward the *Mary*. Were they actually going to sink the boat and drown all those unarmed, innocent passengers?

The shot splashed down off the boat's bow. A cheer went up from the deck. Why were they applauding a miss? He looked at Daniel for an explanation.

"Intentional," he said. "A warning shot. A message to the other crew."

Twenty of the men then knelt at the railing, pistols and muskets loaded and ready to fire. The crew of the *Mary* apparently had no intention of returning that initial shot. In fact, as the *Scurvy Mistress* approached, Fish didn't see much of a crew at all. There were only three men above deck, all standing near the stern.

"What happens now?" Fish asked Daniel.

"I have my role. I stand watch, looking out for other ships. But *you* do nothing. Stay back here, as far from the fight as you can. Otherwise you'll be hurt. Or killed."

The *Scurvy Mistress* drew nearer still. The three men on the *Mary* stood frozen, seemingly ready to submit without a fight. This was an unexpected but welcome development. These were rational men, thought Fish. They measured their own strengths against those of the pirates and decided that a battle between the two forces would be far from even. To prevent the unnecessary loss of lives, they chose to give up rather than fight.

Now they were only thirty feet away. Moravius and three others tossed huge iron hooks tied to long ropes across the water and onto the deck of the other boat. Several more men each grabbed the lines and pulled, bringing the two ships closer. The group of twenty remained poised at the railing, their pistols and muskets ready. The men who'd been polishing their weapons — they must have been the boarders, since Nate stood with them now — crouched behind this larger group, ready to rush. Finally, when only a few feet separated the two boats, the boarders, Nate included, sprang forward and leaped across the gap onto the deck of the *Mary*.

And with that, Fish saw that his assumption about this being a peaceful raid was all wrong. The crew of the *Mary* did not intend to submit without a struggle. They were merely waiting for the ideal moment to strike.

WAR ON THE WATER

As the boarders brandished their blades and pistols, dozens of the *Mary's* men burst out from closed doors and hatches, firing guns and swinging steel. Pistol and musket fire boomed in the air. A cloud of smoke hovered over the decks of both ships. There were shouts and screams of all kinds: rage and triumph, pain and desperation. This was no stage play, no story come to life. These men were fighting viciously.

Fish turned his head away from the scene. Daniel had told him to stay out of the way. And as long as the fighting raged, he would do exactly that. He crouched low on the far side of the boat, clutching his swab as if it might protect him.

The rest of the crew rushed over to assist the boarders. The firing intensified, pistols popping constantly. The smoke thickened. His eyes and throat began burning. Showers of splintered wood erupted into the air as musket balls rammed into the decks and rails of both ships.

Out of the smoke above his head, a dark brown bottle with a flaming cloth stuffed inside crashed to the floor in front of him. Fire leaped up and spread across a small section of the deck. Fish grabbed the soapy bucket of seawater he'd been using to swab and dumped it on the flames.

Dousing the fire renewed his resolve. This was no time to cower in fear; he had to find the purse, get to the other boat, locate Reginald Swift, and, without anyone noticing, slip him the package. Then, since they were still close enough to the shore, he could jump overboard, swim to the coast, and somehow find his way back to the city.

He reached into his pocket, grasped the wooden fish, and turned it over a few times. *Be strong*, he told himself. Coughing, his eyes nearly closed to block out the smoke, he raced down the length of the boat to the captain's cabin, hurried inside, and closed the door.

The battle sounds were muffled in the cabin, the air free of smoke, but it was hardly peaceful. A small, colorful window shattered as a shot burst through. A painting fell to the floor. Be quick, he reminded himself. The next shot could hit you.

In the back corner of the cabin, half hidden behind a pile of locked chests, Fish noticed a small wooden desk with a collection of coins spread out on the surface. Beside them, at the edge of the desk, lay the simple leather purse. His heart thumped in his chest.

Outside, the fight raged. But this was good. The madness was an advantage. It would allow him to slip out again with no difficulty. He stepped to the desk and started to reach for the coins, then froze as someone lifted up the front of his too-large shirt and held a small knife to his stomach.

"With a single slice I can see what you ate for lunch today."

There are a number of ways to react to such a threat. Fish, being nervous, and new to such predicaments, simply said the first thing that came to mind. "But I didn't have any lunch."

His would-be assailant grabbed his shoulder and spun him around. A woman with long red hair stood before him, pointing a knife at his chest.

"What is your name, young man?"

"Fish," he said, his eyes locked on the knife.

"You are new to the crew?"

"Yes." He didn't plan to be part of the crew for long, but she didn't need to know that.

"And they neglected to feed you?"

"Daniel brought me three or four rolls last night. Terribly hard things, like stones. I had a few more after I woke up on deck —"

"You slept on deck? No one provided you with a hammock?"

Someone might have given him a place to sleep if he had chosen to venture below, but again, she didn't need to know such details. Her sympathy could work to his advantage. "No, I —"

"This is an egregious error! A frightful oversight! My husband assured me that we were running a civilized ship, not a boat full of thoughtless brigands!" Dropping the knife to her side, she sat down in a fancily carved wooden chair, one of several in the cabin. "He told me that he would institute the changes I asked for. He told me I would have influence —"

A second window exploded into shards of green and yellow glass. Fish dropped to the floor, but the woman hardly moved. She was annoyed, not frightened. "That was my favorite pane," she lamented.

This shot aside, the battle had lost some of its intensity, and the gunfire had become sporadic. He could have grabbed the coins and run, but the woman looked capable of chasing and pinning him down. She was about his height, thick but not fat. She was healthy and strong, with powerful arms and wide hips, and both elegant and matronly at once. Her narrow eyebrows were so fine they could have been painted on, but her cheeks were full and red with life.

"Melinda Cobb," she said, extending her hand.

"The captain's wife?"

"And much more, in my opinion," she said, smiling. She stood up, walked back over to the desk, and examined the coins. "Intriguing, aren't they?"

He hadn't seen many coins in his life, but these were far more complex than the simple shillings from home. They were full of pictures and symbols; each one harbored enough details and figures to fit a large painting. And, for the most part, they were all different, as if they'd been gathered from points across the globe. But if that were the case, then who had collected them? How had Uncle Gerry become involved? And what did Mr. Swift want with them? Regardless, someone should have tended to them with a little more care, Fish decided. Some of the coins were bright, but the majority were flecked with grime. They demanded the prolonged attention of a good cloth.

A small section of the door splintered, hit from the outside by an errant pistol shot.

"Now," Melinda said, unaffected, "about that lunch." She

hurried over to a closet on the far side of the cabin and opened the door, revealing stacks of packaged food — cartons of biscuits, crackers, tins of salted fish, cheese, and dried meats. "There is one item in here that I'm certain a boy your age would crave," she said, shuffling the cartons and tins from shelf to shelf, "but you'll have to spare me a moment or two. I had this all organized yesterday, but Walter must have gone through it again."

This was his chance. Working hurriedly as she stood with her back to him, Fish swept the coins toward the leather purse. No, that wouldn't do. She'd notice the suddenly bare table and come after him; he wouldn't make it far.

He watched her searching the shelves, mumbling about how her husband had ruined her "system," and ran his hand over his head. The rag! He ripped it off, swept the coins inside, and left the purse in place. Melinda was still mumbling, still scouring. A few steps away he spotted a half-open chest full of gold and silver pieces. He grabbed a handful and, watching Melinda all the while, slowly and quietly spread them across the desk.

Then, gripping the coin-filled rag in one hand, he stepped toward the door.

Over her shoulder Melinda asked, "How about a few biscuits? These are far better than what you'll get below."

She threw one across to Fish. He bit in hungrily and moved to the exit. "Thank you," he said, his mouth half full, "but I should get back to the fight."

Melinda glanced at the desk, squinting at the spread of

coins. Then she tilted her head slightly. "You never told me . . . why were you in here in the first place?"

Fish once again voiced the first thought that came to him. "This place looked safe."

She pulled a pistol out of the closet. He tensed, stopped chewing. But no. She wasn't pointing the weapon at him. She was offering it to him. "This might help you overcome your fear. You'll need it out there."

"No, I won't," Fish answered, and he stepped out onto the deck.

THE SWIFTS

Outside, the smoke had thinned. Cobb's men had subdued the *Mary*'s crew and the battle was over. The boats were tied fast, so Fish crossed easily to the other side.

A group of passengers and sailors were huddled together near the stern. They were frightened and angry, a few of them bleeding and bandaged, and Reginald Swift was not among them. He had to be down below, so Fish descended.

The *Mary* was three times as large as the *Scurvy Mistress*. The lower decks were a maze of narrow corridors and small closed doors. The pirates were shoving and pushing two, three, four passengers at a time down the main hall toward a large central cabin. Fish had no idea how he was going to find a single man down there, let alone an uncommonly small one. The boat was big enough to fit several hundred people, and Reginald Swift was small enough to cram himself into a closet.

But then he realized he didn't have to find Swift. At least not right away. If he were to hide somewhere until the men from the *Scurvy Mistress* plundered the boat and sailed off, he could safely find him after they'd gone. The crew of the *Mary* would probably reward his heroics by sailing him back to the city. Even dropping him closer to shore would be payment enough. Either way, he could return to Uncle Gerry triumphant.

With this in mind, he hurried down the main hall, chose a slightly open door to his left, then fell onto his back as Scab, with his black eyes gleaming and his squat face flashing a wicked smile of cracked teeth, burst out with a handful of jewels. "Move along, worm!" he shouted, and pushed Fish down the hall.

They came to a wide open room with tables lined up throughout. Fish held tight to the bundle of coins. He was not going to lose them again.

At least fifty passengers were bunched on one side. There must have been twenty pirates from the *Scurvy Mistress* down there, too, all with pistols and cutlasses drawn. Thimble was walking among them, drinking from a bottle of wine, wrapping wounds with spare rags. He had passed one of the *Mary*'s sailors, a young man who was bleeding from a blow to his head, when Cobb called out to him. "*All* of the wounded, Thimble, not merely our own."

The red-faced pirate snorted, rolled his small eyes, took another swig, and returned to the bleeding sailor.

A fat, bearded man, kneeling on the floor, pleaded for the rogues to leave him alone. Instead of granting his request, Scab calmly walked over and walloped him with the butt of his pistol. The man crumpled.

Another passenger, a younger, more fit man, protested in response. Nate rushed over and lifted his own pistol to strike him, but before he could bring the weapon down, Cobb grabbed his wrist, stared hard into the boy's eyes. "We are not animals. Victory is ours. We must now turn to more important matters."

He released Nate's arm, leaned against a table with Moravius on one side and Scab on the other. Before them, an old woman, old enough to be Fish's grandmother, sat in a chair. Her white, curly hair was pulled up in a bun. Her face was so pale and wrinkled that she could have passed for a ghost. But her eyes, blue and bright, sparked with life.

At first, the giant was blocking Fish's view, but when Moravius moved, he saw a man kneeling beside her. No, he wasn't kneeling at all. He was, Fish realized, uncommonly small.

"Tell me where you've hidden your riches, and we will spare you and the rest of these fine, innocent passengers," Cobb said.

The woman's gaze was venomous. "Don't you already have what you came for, Cobb?"

"We know that you are transporting a sizeable portion of your fortune on this boat, Swift —"

"Lady Swift," the old woman snapped.

She had to be Reginald's mother, Fish guessed — the one he'd referred to on the dock.

"By whose order? The queen?"

"I need no queen to achieve my title. I am Lady Swift because I say so."

"Very well, Lady Swift. We would like to relieve you of those monies in a civilized way. Will you allow us that courtesy?

Since you are, as you insist, a lady, I imagine you will allow us to conduct ourselves like gentlemen?"

"You are not gentlemen. You are scoundrels!" she yelled.

Reginald Swift spat on the floor. This was clearly an attempt to express solidarity, but the diminutive glob of saliva wasn't terribly offensive. Even the man's spit was tiny.

Scab laughed and planted a massive wad next to Swift's paltry effort.

"Reginald, please!" Lady Swift shouted. "If you must attempt to assert yourself amidst these ruffians, try to be more effective. Otherwise, just stand there like a good boy."

"But, Mother, I —"

"Quiet! And as for you, Cobb, I'll die before giving you the scantest clue."

Teeth clenched, Cobb breathed in slowly through his long nose and traced the single scar on his chin with one of his slender fingers. The gesture calmed him; a moment earlier, he had looked ready to strike the old woman.

Scab had no such reserve. He rushed in, slapped Reginald Swift across the face with one of his thick, yellowed hands, then held a knife to the man's thin, clean-shaven throat. "Will you tell us now?" he asked the old woman.

Although Cobb's attempt to interrogate Lady Swift proved ineffective, Scab's worked quite well. She might have been perfectly willing to belittle her son, but apparently she did value his life. Seeing the blade at his throat and the obvious taste for violence in Scab's face, Lady Swift pointed toward a huge stack of barrels lined up against the wall. The words printed on the front varied: SALTED PORK, BUTTER, BISCUITS, BEER, and more.

This didn't strike Fish as particularly exciting treasure. It would have to be very delicious food, considering all the difficulties these pirates had endured to secure it.

"In one of those barrels?" Cobb asked.

"Correct."

"Which one?" Scab demanded.

Lady Swift sneered. Her wrinkles deepened. "Find it yourself."

Scab wrapped his hand around her son's throat and the woman gave in once more, pointing directly at a barrel labeled PEPPERS. Cobb nodded to Moravius, who slammed the barrel to the floor, releasing the lid and a pile of gold coins. "Gather it all," Cobb called to his men. "Gather it all and return to the boat."

The crew cheered, but Lady Swift yelled at the captain. "You will never find it, you know. You have neither the patience nor the intelligence. You are too weak."

Most of the men ignored the lady's words. They were busy collecting the coins. But Scab heard her. "Find what?" he asked.

"Nothing," Cobb replied. "She is a mad old woman. Please dispense with her and her diminutive son."

"Kill them?"

"No. Lock them away so I don't have to hear that decrepit woman's voice any longer."

Scab grabbed Reginald Swift by the collar. Lady Swift,

noting the tension between the captain and his first mate, began to smile. She stood up, clasped Scab's arm above the elbow, whispered something in his ear, then walked off at his side as if he were leading her into a ball.

Cobb watched them momentarily, then shook his head and began directing the men.

Fish crept after Scab and the Swifts. He could have chosen to hide, as he'd planned before, and then hand over the coins once the pirates had gone, but he decided instead to heed one of his uncle Gerry's rules: Never save a task for tomorrow if it can be completed today. Besides, Reginald Swift needed the good news.

The trio disappeared down a long, narrow hallway. He walked slowly, quietly, and heard voices coming from the other side of a slightly opened door.

"Reginald," he heard Lady Swift say, "please step out. This conversation is for professionals."

"But, Mother, you told me I would be allowed to take part in all the —"

"And I have changed my mind. Now wait outside like a good boy."

The door swung open. Eyes downcast, muttering, Reginald Swift stepped into the hall. "I'm not a boy," he said in a near whisper. "I'm nearly thirty years old! Yet she treats me —" He saw Fish and nearly gasped. "You!"

"All is not lost," Fish said.

Swift's eyes brightened behind his giant glasses. "Quiet!"

he whispered, glancing furtively down the hall, checking to see if anyone was watching them speak. "Show me."

Fish unraveled the rag and showed him the coins. Swift's eyes grew as wide as his spectacles. "Ha! She can't call me useless now. I recovered the coins, not her!" He pressed Fish's closed hands joyfully. "And the purse?"

"I don't have it," Fish said. "I had to smuggle them out this way."

Reginald Swift slammed his small fist against the wall. "The clue . . . the purse . . . what's the use . . . you stupid boy!"

His small shoulders sagged. Obviously Swift had no idea what Fish had gone through to get him these coins. He had risked his life more than once. But instead of thanking him, Reginald Swift was angry.

Fish was annoyed, but tried to remain respectful. "I apologize, but this is the best I could do. Will you take them?"

Mr. Swift didn't answer.

"No," Cobb said from behind him. "I will."

The captain held out his hand. Melinda, her face as red as her hair, stood at his side. A sickening feeling spread outward from Fish's center, as though he'd been punched in the stomach. Defeat; he'd never get the coins back from the captain. And as for Melinda, he could hardly look at her. She'd been perfectly kind to him, even feeding him, and he had cheated her. He felt terrible. About everything.

Hands shaking, he passed the coins to Cobb.

Scab must have heard the captain; he stepped out into the hall. In the cabin, Lady Swift sat calmly in a chair. Cobb glowered at her, then turned to her son. "Inside with your mother. Now, Mr. Swift."

"Captain!" Daniel shouted, running toward them down the hall. "Another ship is approaching!"

"Navy?"

"No," Daniel said. "A sloop, from the looks of her. New, bright white sails, but the rest of her appears aged. She's a good distance away but gaining."

"Let her be," Scab suggested.

"Is your hunger for battle sated?" Cobb asked.

"We've had enough fight today."

"Precisely," Cobb replied, appearing surprised that he and his normally war-hungry first mate were in agreement. "Transfer what bounty you can and hoist the sails. We will have no more battles today. The time has come for us to venture into the blue desert."

The blue desert? He had to mean the ocean. Fish took a few steps back. This would be his last chance to get back to the city, or even home. If he could just hide . . .

"Oh, no, boy," Cobb said, grabbing his too-large shirt. "You are not slithering off. You have questions to answer."

Saving the Enemy

The *Scurvy Mistress* sailed away, leaving the battered *Mary*, her passengers, and the mystery sloop in her wake. Any hope of completing his task was now gone. And Fish had been so close! Now he would lose his position with Uncle Gerry. He'd be sent home, where he'd be met with half smiles and reluctant embraces. His brothers' punches wouldn't be affectionate; they'd probably try to wallop him for real. He was not going back to that.

At that moment, in fact, Fish was not going anywhere. Cobb had ordered one of the pirates, whose name was Knot, to bind him to the railing. The man did so with amazing speed and dexterity; Fish's hands were tied up behind him mere seconds after he sat down.

The crew was going through the process of recording the various trinkets, coins, and treasures plundered from the *Mary*. The men stood in a line, their pockets stuffed, some of them carrying or carting small chests, and one by one handed their haul to an old, gray-haired, blade-thin man with an unusually long head and a pointy chin. He studied each item closely, then handed it to one of a pair of pirates behind him, who stored everything in a collection of small barrels.

That must be the purser, Fish thought. He'd met plenty of them in the city; on normal boats, they kept track of supplies, but on a pirate ship, apparently, they were charged with the added task of tallying loot.

"His name is Foot."

The sun had just burned through the clouds, and the glare made it difficult to see, but from the voice he knew it was Daniel.

"He's the purser?" Fish asked.

"That's right. Hardly ever speaks a word, let alone a sentence, but he is a right wizard with numbers. Notice how he doesn't even keep a ledger?"

That was odd, Fish thought. Usually the pursers he dealt with always had a ledger and pencil on hand.

"Has no need for one." Daniel tapped his head. "Keeps it all up here. They say he doesn't speak because he doesn't have any room for words in his head, with all the numbers stored in there. We call him Foot because his right foot is probably the foulest-smelling thing on the ocean. He's been wearing the same boot for decades. The left one he changes three or four times a year, but not the right one. He says it helps him think. And it might, given the fact that he's always tapping it when he's adding up numbers, like a fiddler keeping a beat. Always the right foot, never the left."

Daniel was correct; the man's right foot, shod in a heavily worn brown boot, was practically bouncing on the deck.

"So what did you do to get yourself in that bind?" Daniel asked, pointing to Fish's tied-up hands. "Did you try to steal from the captain or something?"

"No!" Fish insisted. "They were my coins. Or I was supposed to deliver them, anyway."

"You did steal from the captain, didn't you? Have you been drinking seawater? If there's one person you need to respect, it's the captain. But hey, you've probably got it better than Nate the Great. He did the only thing worse than stealing from the captain."

"What's that?"

"He stole from the crew. During the raid, he grabbed a few armfuls of loot but tried to keep one item, a necklace, for himself. Didn't hand it to Foot when his turn came. Can't figure out why, either, since the thing didn't look to be worth all that much — merely a bit of silver with a few cheap stones."

"Why is he being punished if it wasn't worth anything?" Fish asked.

"Why?! It's against our rules, our code, our entire way of life! When we take a prize, everything, and I mean every last trinket, from a golden bracelet to an old silver fork, goes to Foot, who divides it up, all of it, among the crew."

"So that necklace was as much yours as it was his?"

"Right. More importantly, in terms of old Nate the Great's fate, it belonged to Scab, Thimble, and the rest of the roughest part of the crew, too. Once Scab found out about the necklace, Nate was finished. You can tell Cobb isn't too happy about having to do it. I think he had some faith in Nate. Thought he'd make a good captain one day. But rules are rules."

"What are they going to do to him?" Fish asked.

Now Daniel pointed toward the bow, where the men began to convene as the last of them deposited their hauls with Foot. With the accounting complete, they were ready to turn to Nate's sentence. Cobb and Moravius remained near the stern, unwilling or unable to watch. The captain was not pleased with what was about to take place, but he wasn't about to halt it, either. "What are they going to do to him?" he asked again.

Daniel pulled a medallion out from under his shirt, kissed it twice quickly, then said, "They're making him walk the plank."

"Won't he swim to shore?"

"Pirates don't swim," Daniel answered. "Or at least, not well enough to get all the way to the shore. Walking the plank," he said, "is a death sentence."

Death? Fish felt suddenly cold. He understood the importance of rules, but death was an unjustly permanent punishment for such a small theft.

A group of pirates pushed a one-foot-wide, extremely long plank of wood through a short opening beneath the railing on the far side of the ship. They secured one end by rolling one of the treasure-laden barrels on top of it. The other end stretched out some fifteen feet from the side of the boat and hung over the sea.

The men mostly stood with their backs to Fish, but even without seeing their faces, he could tell this was not a proud or joyous moment for most. They stood stiff and strong, unhappy to send one of their crew to the depths, especially such a young one, but certain of the sentence, too, given that he had stolen from them.

There were a few exceptions to the somber mood. Scab and Thimble were smiling, along with a man who was bald but for a horseshoe of brown hair wrapping around his head from ear level down. They regarded the proceedings as entertainment.

Nate walked to the edge of the board, then turned to face the crew.

Scab, stifling laughter, shouted, "Any last words?"

Nate gulped. "I had my reasons for taking the necklace," he began in a quivering voice. "None of which had to do with greed."

Fish noticed that Nate's gaze shifted to the back of the crowd. A girl was standing there. She was dressed in a ragged, dirty dress, yet she was most certainly a girl. He hadn't seen her before; she definitely hadn't been up on the deck.

When Nate looked at her, she lowered her head. "But I was wrong," he continued. "Wrong to steal from my crew. My brothers. My family."

Several more men averted their eyes, too pained to watch. Why they were letting this proceed if they didn't really want it to, Fish could not understand. Surely they could make an exception.

Finally, Nate said, "I accept my fate," and he fell backward into the sea.

Daniel lifted the medallion to his lips and kissed it twice more.

The initial splash was loud, and smaller ones followed. Most of the crew stepped away from the railing. Thimble, Scab, and a few others leaned over the edge, pointing and laughing. Fish could hear Nate struggling, gasping for air and swallowing water.

The other men might let Nate drown, but Fish was not going to live by their brutal rules. He was going to save the boy.

There was still one problem, though. His hands. "Daniel," he said, "cut me loose!"

"What?"

"I'm going to save him," Fish said, struggling against the ropes, attempting to wriggle out on his own. For once, he was thankful for his small hands. The ropes were loosening; he might be able to slip out.

"But you can't save somebody who's been ordered to —"

"He made a mistake!" Fish said, his fingers working furiously on the knot. One of the loops was giving way. "You heard him. He admitted it. Shouldn't that be enough? Wouldn't you want another chance?"

"Yes, I suppose so, but . . ."

The knot loosened. Fish pulled harder. The skin of his wrists was burning and his hands ached. Yet it was working. One hand slipped through, then the next. He was free.

"Forget I asked," he said.

A few seconds later, he leaped over the railing of the *Scurvy Mistress* and dove into the water below. He surfaced, spotted the doomed young pirate start to sink just a few strokes away.

Fish raced over to Nate, slipped his arm across the half-drowned boy's chest, and dragged him up to the surface.

"You can't save him!" someone yelled from above.

"That's not allowed!"

"Let him drown!" another pirate added.

But not all of the men stood against him. A few other crew members were cheering; Daniel was clapping in appreciation.

Cobb came to the edge. "Bring them up!" he ordered. "Bring them both up."

A rope ladder dropped down into the water. Fish swam over, breathing heavily, held Nate afloat, and grabbed onto it. Still coughing, confused that he wasn't dead and drowned, Nate slowly climbed the ladder. Fish followed. Halfway up, he looked back toward the shore. A fog had gathered along the coast; he could no longer see beyond the beach. Ireland was disappearing from view.

INTERROGATION

Cold, wet, and hungry, Fish sat in a chair in the captain's cabin. Though this was his second visit, he hadn't really studied it earlier that day, as he'd been concentrating on the coins. Small but colorful windows, two of which had been boarded up after the raid, lined three of the walls; they reminded him of church. Several great chests lay about, most of them closed and locked tight, a few propped open and overflowing with coins and long strings of pearls. There were numerous paintings, too, all featuring pastoral scenes of farms, cows grazing in green meadows, sheep lazing on hilltops. This was surprising; he would have expected sailing ships and stormy, wind-crazed seas.

They were kind enough to provide him with a blanket, but there were no offers of warm milk or food, despite the fact that he was starved. He would have happily eaten a dozen of those rock-hard rolls he'd munched on for breakfast.

The mood in the cabin was tense. Melinda stood in a far corner, too furious with him to come any closer, her thin eyebrows slanting angrily in and down. Cobb paced behind Fish, puffing intensely on a tobacco pipe. The giant was with them, too, and although he looked pensive, someone who made rooster noises couldn't have been thinking anything too profound.

Fish had been trying to convince them that he was just a messenger, that he was merely intent on completing his assigned task, but they did not believe him. They had other, grander notions.

"You tell me to trust you," Cobb said, "but I do not see how this is possible. You tried to steal from us."

"You betrayed my trust," Melinda added.

"But I had a responsibility —"

"Yes, yes, we've heard all about that," Cobb said. "I applaud your sense of responsibility. It is a respectable quality in a boy. Our difficulty, though, is ensuring that your responsibilities, your loyalties, now lie with me and my crew." A circular rack of tobacco pipes sat on Cobb's desk. He spun it, watching the pipe stems turn. "How do I know you're not a spy?"

Fish laughed. The very idea was insane.

"You snuck into my cabin," Cobb said.

"But I was —"

"You studied my personal items."

"I was looking for —"

"You stole precious coins and attempted to deliver them to one of our chief competitors, a very famous and successful treasure hunter."

"Reginald Swift is a treasure hunter?"

"His mother, Lady Swift, commands the operation, but he is involved. Yet I am certain you know that already. Do not play the part of simpleton with us. Tell me now: Do you work directly for the Swifts? If not, who is your employer?"

Former employer would be more accurate — Uncle Gerry would never give him his old position back. But Cobb wouldn't care about that. "Reidy Merchants," he answered at last.

"Known traffickers of treasure-related information," Melinda said.

Again Fish laughed. Of all the accusations, this one had to be the most absurd. "That is ridiculous," he said. "Uncle Gerry is a merchant. He is not the sort to be involved with pirates and treasure hunters."

"Wrong! Incorrect! Mistaken! That purse, which was in his possession, is a critical clue —"

A small coin hit Cobb in the head. The giant looked away, scratching his large, crooked nose. He had obviously thrown it. Perhaps Moravius could follow some of their conversation. But if so, why was he silent?

Cobb stopped mid-sentence and scratched the spot where he'd been hit. His thick curls moved in unison. A wig! Of course. Fish should have known he was wearing a wig.

"Never mind the coins," Cobb continued. "Both your behavior and your allegiances suggest that you are not someone to be trusted."

Fish tried not to dwell on the notion that his uncle Gerry conducted business with pirates. Somehow he needed to convince Cobb that he was not a spy. Surely his rescue of Nate meant something. And he had saved Scab, too. "But I did prevent two of your men from drowning. Why would I do that if I was working for someone else?"

"To sow the seeds of mutiny!" Cobb responded. "A ship like ours can only function if all the men aboard agree to adhere to a set of rules. I can honestly find nothing sensible in your effort to save Scab, but in rescuing Nathaniel, you made those rules appear less absolute. I cannot tolerate this dissent. If the crew suspects that our rules are not burned into the very hull of this ship, they will bend, circumvent, and break them. They could very well decide to overturn my leadership."

The captain's wig slipped slightly; he fidgeted with it for a moment, then stopped, satisfied. Why a man would wear such a thing on his head, Fish could not understand. It looked like it should have been used to clean floors or scrub pots.

Fish caught Melinda rolling her eyes. "A touch dramatic, Walter. You were the one who decided that Nate could live."

"But that was perfectly reasonable! The rules say that thieves must walk the plank. Nathaniel *did* walk the plank." Holding out the stem of his pipe, the captain added, "The rules don't say he has to die."

"Nonetheless, you can't blame our young spy here for your own decisions."

"I am not a spy!" Fish declared, slamming his small fist down on the arm of the chair. "I saved him because it is cruel to let someone drown over a necklace. Nate made a mistake and he apologized. That should have been enough." He waited for them to respond. They remained silent, staring at him. Perhaps he was convincing them. "If it's not," Fish continued, "then I don't believe I want to be part of your crew, Captain Cobb. I don't want to count myself a member of a group that applauds violence and death. And it's not only Nate. The beatings some of your men delivered aboard the *Mary* . . . that was far from respectable behavior."

They were quiet. Had he been too assertive? Perhaps he should have left that last part out. He should have considered the possibility that talking to the captain in this manner would earn him a beating of his own. Yet even though Cobb was the leader of so many brutal men, the captain himself didn't seem like a violent person. He certainly wasn't like that vicious beast Scab.

"Young man," Cobb responded, "I would prefer it if we never raided another ship. Unfortunately, this would all but ensure mutiny. If the men do not accumulate riches at a steady pace, my control of the *Scurvy Mistress* will not last long, even if she *is* my sloop."

"I don't understand," Fish said. "If you are the captain, don't they have to do as you say?"

"On a traditional vessel, perhaps," Cobb answered. "But we operate outside the bounds of traditional rules and regulations. A pirate ship is a different sort of society, boy. The captain is only in control for as long as the majority of the crew desires."

"What happens if they don't want you to be captain anymore?"

"With hope we will never discover that. For now, though, I hold sway over the majority of the men. Their interests are aligned with mine. Yet a number of our sailors, and a handful of very valuable and useful ones at that, lack the patience for the sort of quest I prefer. They need to be appeased with raids and robberies of the kind we conducted today."

"Like Scab?" Fish asked.

"Yes. All pirates seek wealth and fortune, but some prefer a different means of acquiring it. There are raiders, like Scab, who believe that storming and attacking any and every ship that crosses one's path is the swiftest and surest route to fortune. And then there are seekers, such as Melinda and myself, who prefer a more challenging quest in search of even greater riches."

"You already have quite a store here. . . ."

"No, boy," Cobb said. "We seek far grander prizes. I speak of treasures that will render the coins in these chests as worthless as pebbles and stones."

Fish imagined having his own chest full of gold and jewels. The coins would shine like the surface of a sunstruck lake, strings of white pearls would lie coiled beneath green emeralds as big as his fists. He'd send the treasure back home to provide for his family. He'd be rich, as Daniel had said. That is, assuming that he would receive a fair portion. "Does everyone share in what you find?" he asked.

"Not evenly, but yes, of course. Every member of the crew receives his or her share."

"Would it be enough to buy a horse?"

Cobb and Melinda laughed; even the giant smiled.

"A herd of horses, my boy!" Cobb answered.

The captain struck a match and refired his pipe, sucked in deeply, and puffed out the thick smoke. Fish considered what to do. They might still be within range of the shore; after he rescued Nate, he had heard one of the men say they would follow the coast for another day. But why swim back? Uncle Gerry wouldn't have him. His parents would welcome him home, but he didn't want to return to the farm ragged and penniless.

No, they sent him away so that he could earn money. They placed their faith in him and he would not disappoint them. He would not buy them one horse, but a herd!

Granted, the life of a seafaring adventurer would bear no comparison to that of a messenger. The work would be more dangerous, more difficult, the days longer. But he'd already made one friend in Daniel, which was more than he had in the city. And the lure of a quest was far more exciting than anything he'd done before.

Yes, he was sure of it. The choice was simple. He would become a treasure hunter.

Before he could announce his decision, Cobb spoke. "You could earn great riches, but if you wish to earn a share aboard this sloop, you will first need to convince us, once and for all, that you are not a spy."

Now Fish's face grew hot; he clenched his teeth. What was he supposed to do? Swear on his mother's name? No, words would not be enough. They did not trust him and he had to change this. But how?

His fingers caressed the small, carved fish in his pocket. The wood had become smoother in the months since Roisin had given it to him; he rubbed it constantly for comfort. It would hurt to give it up, but this was the only way he could think of to convince Cobb to trust him. Fish would give him his most treasured possession.

He pulled it out of his pocket, held it before him, and stared up at the captain. He looked one last time at the small carving, the only physical reminder of the life he was planning to leave behind, then flicked it through the air to Cobb.

The captain caught the fish and inspected it briefly. He was not impressed. "What is this?"

"My sister gave it to me when I left," Fish explained. "I know it isn't much. It does not compare to the treasures you have here. But it is all I have, besides these wet and worn clothes. It is my single and most valuable possession, and I am giving it to you."

"Might I ask why?"

"Because you are my captain. All that I have is yours, and that fish is all that I have. Consider it a pledge of loyalty. A pledge of my faith."

Cobb glanced at his wife and the giant, then smiled at Fish and tossed him the carving. "We are your family now. Welcome aboard, Fish."

HELL'S KITCHEN

Though Fish was hoping the captain would invite him to dine with them, he was ushered out of the cabin once Cobb granted him an official position on the boat. A bell chimed, and Cobb ordered him belowdecks for his dinner. The place still frightened him, but there would be no arguing about it now — he descended immediately.

The pirates ate and slept in a single large cabin that ran roughly half the length of the ship. This would be his dining room, his bedroom, and his workplace. His chief responsibility on the *Scurvy Mistress* would be to swab and scrub the cabin clean.

The job sounded appealing until Fish actually saw the place. First, it was nothing like the captain's cabin. There were no tables, no desks, no paintings or chests overflowing with treasure. Against both walls, huge black cannons sat secured by thick ropes. Hammocks hung from the ceiling. Chunks of green, moldy meat and cheese were stuck to the walls and floor. The smell of rotting food and dirty men assaulted his nose like a hundred punches. Fish was raised on a farm, so he did have experience with revolting smells. He had shoveled and stepped in gargantuan piles of cow manure, and he once spent several months tending to the family's three fat and foul pigs. Yet this room . . . he could find no word to describe the singular potency of its smell.

As Fish stood at the bottom of the stairs, nose scrunched to avoid taking in too much of the air, one of the pirates approached him. He was about Fish's height but a decade older, with thinning hair, forearms as large as his legs, and a pair of spectacles tucked into his shirt pocket. His eyes, Fish decided, were too close together, and his prominent jaw culminated in a very small chin. He rubbed that tiny chin before saying, "Putrocious, no?"

"Excuse me?" Fish asked. He'd never heard the word before.

"Putrocious," the man repeated. "It's an invention of mine. The word, that is. I believe no other arrangement of letters in the English language quite captures the stench down here, so I created that word myself, by fusing 'putrid' and 'atrocious.' For some time I thought 'stindiferous' applied well enough, but I have since decided otherwise." The man waited, as if he was allowing Fish a moment to appreciate the genius of his very strange words. Then he held out his hand. "The name is Simon."

They shook. "Fish," he said.

"Fair winds to you, Fish." Simon pulled a worn, yellowed journal from his back pocket. "Filled with my own lexical concoctions. A few more raids and I will have enough money to have it published in London."

Fish briefly examined the book, but the noise and smells

quickly drew his attention back to the cabin. There must have been thirty or forty men packed inside — Daniel and Nate, the only other boys, were nowhere in sight. Some of the pirates stood, some sat on the floor in groups of five or six, eating from small bowls and drinking from massive mugs. The air was hot and thick, the noise incredibly loud, as if an entire city had been stuffed into a single room.

"Frightening bunch, eh?" Simon said.

"Terrifying," Fish answered.

"I assure you we are less intimidating once you grow to know us. We are creatures of habit, the lot of us. Or crabits, if you will. That group, there" — he pointed to a circle of rotund men, their cheeks and necks bursting with fat — "they call themselves the Scalawags for Sausage. Their main goal in this waterlogged life is to see to it that their bellies are filled with salted meats. Their leader is Sammy the Stomach, the one with the biggest belly —"

Fish remembered Daniel talking about him. "An accomplished gunner?"

"Correct! Next to him, the old fellows with the eye patches, those would be the One-eyed Willies. A depressing bunch, really. I'd avoid supping with them if you can, as all they do is talk about their missing eyes, lamenting their loss of depth perception. The Tea Leaves, those well-dressed fellows in the corner, they're all British, ex–Royal Navy men. A more superior-feeling bunch of sailors you'll never meet. You'd do well to sit with the Over and Unders, the gents working with the ropes. They're not great for conversation, since all they do is tie and untie their knots, but you might learn a trick or two about their trade, which can be a useful thing on a ship."

He recognized Knot, the man who'd tied him up earlier in the day, and, in a larger group behind the Over and Unders, Scab and Thimble, the fancily dressed tailor. "And them?" Fish asked.

"Rascals, every one," Simon answered. "Bound only by an unmatched hunger for gold and a steady thirst for blood. They'd kill their mothers for an extra doubloon."

Fish took note of each man in the group and reminded himself to avoid them entirely. "How about yourself?" he asked. "Where do you fit in?"

"Indetonomous. Independent and autonomous; I keep to my words and my work. No affiliations. Friends with everyone, enemies to no one. I'll eat with the Scalawags one day, the Over and Unders the next. I would suggest that you do the same . . . and speaking of eating, have you had your grub?"

"No."

"Now is the time," Simon answered, and pointed over his shoulder toward a small counter. A few men were in line, each holding a bowl. The girl from the deck, the one who had been watching as Nate walked the plank, stood on the other side of the counter, inside the small galley, ladling what looked like soup out of a large pot. "Thank you, I think I will," Fish said.

"Verycome," Simon answered. "That's —"

"Wait, let me guess. Very welcome?"

"Right! Enjoy your gruel."

Fish summoned a dash of courage, said a quick prayer that no one would strike him, and walked to the counter.

"What will it be?" the girl asked.

Fish was staring, unintentionally, at her eyes. They were a very familiar shade of green, the color of a pasture in spring. He'd never seen eyes so odd.

"I said, 'What will it be?'"

Fish rubbed his eyes like a man who'd just been woken from a nap. "Excuse me?"

"To eat. What would you like to eat?"

If she were giving him a choice, then some nice soft bread with butter and a few warm potatoes would be ideal. Perhaps a glass of milk, too.

The girl laughed. "I'm only jesting. You have two choices," she said, lifting the lid of the large, blackened pot behind the counter to reveal a grayish-green, steaming sludge. "Gruel, and gruel with hardtack."

"Hardtack?"

"Biscuits, baked nearly before you and I were born. Hard as stones if you bite into them plain, but if you break them up a bit, crumble them into your gruel, and mix them around, they might not crack any of your teeth."

"Butter?"

"A luxury. This journey will be a long one. Six to eight weeks, I'd guess, and that means we have to conserve. You won't taste any butter for quite a while. The diet here is simple, really. Gruel and hardtack at night. A piece of meat once a day and some hard cheese, too. Gruel and a glass of goat's milk in the morning —"

"You have goats on board?"

"Yes. And hens, too, all down below this deck." The girl stopped stirring the gruel and studied Fish for a moment. "Look at you," she said. "Pale, unwrinkled skin." She reached over the counter and took his hands. "Palms that have never seen true toil. Eyes that haven't witnessed the dark side of the world. You haven't been to sea before, have you?"

"No," Fish answered, pulling his hands away. He closed them into fists. Why did everyone keep looking at his hands? And what did she mean about his eyes never having seen the dark side of the world? Fish had lived in a city. And three times in the past two days, someone had pressed a knife to his skin. He didn't appreciate being regarded as an innocent child. There was more to him than that — and he would show her. He would show all of them.

His stomach grumbled. He would show them later. After he ate.

"You sound Irish," she continued, ignoring his hungry stare at the gruel. "Grew up in Dublin, I presume? Attended a fancy school, waited on by servants? Then you ran away from home for a life of adventure and found yourself here, wishing you'd never left."

"No, no, no!" Fish snapped. These people and their assumptions were infuriating. First Cobb, and now her. "I was raised on a farm and sent off to work because Shamrock — that's our horse — died. Now I'm here, hoping to earn my share and do what I can to help my family. But most of all I'm hungry. I need food. And whether it's plain gruel or gruel with crack-your-teeth biscuit, I would very much appreciate it if you would serve me some. Please."

The girl's head pitched forward. "What did you say?"

"I said I'm hungry and —"

"No," she said, waving her hand, "after that."

" 'Please'?"

"That's right! You did say it! Please!" A smile as bright as any he'd ever seen lit up her face. "Please!" she repeated. "No one has said 'please' to me in" — she stopped, started counting on her fingers — "six months! I'm Nora," she announced, and passed him a bowl and some hardtack.

He dropped in the hardened biscuit and spooned some of the gruel into his mouth. The texture of it was unpleasant — more muddy than creamy — and it had an unexpected tang that suggested at least one of the ingredients had spoiled. Still, he swallowed the stuff, and another spoonful after that.

"I know it's not good, but it's the best I can do with what we have," Nora said. "Every second day I'll add some chicken to the gruel. When we get to the islands, we'll have turtles, too."

Closing his eyes, Fish took in another mouthful. He tried to imagine that it was one of his mother's soups, with fresh potatoes and vegetables. This improved the experience slightly, allowing him to swallow down a few more spoonfuls.

Unfortunately, though, the thought of those meals brought up a chain of memories: of his mother, his sisters and brothers, and of how his father looked at him when he left him with Uncle Gerry. His father loved him. Fish knew that. His father didn't want to leave him in the city — he simply had no choice.

The thought of home shook him. Perhaps he hadn't made the right decision after all. Perhaps he should have jumped off the boat when he had the chance.

Fish clenched his teeth. No. He was almost twelve years old and he had responsibilities. He had to show this girl, and the rest of the crew, that he was strong. That he was prepared for what life on the ocean was going to blow his way.

Nora was staring at him expectantly, the way his mother used to look at his father after she'd put a special effort into one of her meals. She was hoping for a compliment. Fish thought hard, searching his mind for something nice to say. "Ummm . . . it's warm . . . and filling."

"Don't lie. I can see you're not impressed. But I *can* cook. And I'll prove it to you. Check to see if anyone's looking."

"No," he said, seeing that they were all focused on either their gruel or the drinks in their enormous mugs. "All busy."

Nora dropped down to her knee, opened a small hatch below the counter, and waved him in. The opening was barely large enough for him to fit through. "Stay down," she said. "Normally I don't allow anyone back here, so we can't let the other scoundrels see you."

She reached down to take Fish's hand and led him, crawling, to a door at the back of the room. Her hand, though far rougher than his own, was warm and thin. He felt his face redden; he'd held his sisters' hands before, but never that of a girl he'd just met.

Nora opened the door, pulled Fish through, and closed it behind them. "Go ahead, you can stand up now."

There were stacks of boxes and barrels behind her, filled with flour and biscuits and beer and wine, plus a few crates of wilting vegetables. Over her left shoulder a few dead, feather-less chickens were hanging from a long rope. To her right, coal burned in a small stove. A large, battered pot sat atop the stove; Nora removed the top, pulled a rusty metal ladle from a hook on the wall, and stirred the boiling contents. More gruel.

"You feed everybody from here?"

"Everybody but the captain and his wife. On most pirate ships, the captain eats with the rest of the men, but not on the *Scurvy Mistress*. Cobb and his wife cook together and pride themselves on their talents. But I promise you that if given the right ingredients, I could produce the best meal he has had in his life." She rolled a small barrel away from one of the walls, revealing a tiny wooden panel. "Don't tell anyone about this."

"I won't."

Nora opened the panel, stuck her hand inside, and moved around some of the contents. After a bit of searching, she pulled out a small log of salami and a brick of hard, yellowish-white cheese. She searched further and produced three jars, each filled with sliced vegetables soaking in greenish water.

From a cabinet beside the stove she removed a loaf of bread. Then she reached up the sleeve of her shirt and removed a long, thin, gleaming knife. Fish stepped back. Two days on a pirate ship had already taught him that when someone unsheathed a blade, you moved.

"No, no," Nora said, lowering the knife. "It's for cooking."

"So why do you hide it in your sleeve?"

Nora began slicing the hardened bread, the cheese, and the salted meat. "It's not only for cooking, but protection, too," she answered. "I'm thirteen years old, and a girl. Cobb has his rules, but I still need to be on my guard. So I've taught myself to be good with knives." She revealed another, tucked up her right sleeve, then a third and fourth strapped to her ankles. "That is less than half of them."

She placed two slices of bread over the hot stove, cut the cheese and salami into thin pieces, and then removed a few unappetizing items from the jars. Fish covered his nose.

"Pickled vegetables," she said. "Please withhold judgment until you've tried one."

This food was interesting, but Fish wanted to know more about Nora's knives. "Have you ever had to use one? On another person, I mean."

"Once or twice," Nora answered, flipping the two pieces of bread on the stove. "A few of the scars on this boat are my handiwork. But now the men know to avoid me."

"How did you end up here?"

"My mother died, and my father, whom I never met, wrote me a letter informing me that he would be glad to support me if I had been a boy, but that he could not raise a girl. So I decided to become a boy. I changed my clothes and learned to fight and talk like a boy. But the best way to truly become one was to go to sea."

"You don't look much like a boy now," Fish noted.

Not in the slightest, in fact. Her green eyes were shielded by thick, long lashes. Her skin was bone white, her hair long and blond. If forced to identify a flaw, he might only say that her nose was mildly upturned, but this gave her a slightly regal air, suggesting that she did not belong in the belly of this boat, but in its most important cabin. A potent and not very ladylike smell surrounded her, too, but Fish decided that it came from the gruel, not the girl.

"No, I gave up on that shortly after we set to sea. I saw the *Scurvy Mistress* down at the dock one day, and she was calling herself a paperless privateer —"

"Which is another name for a pirate, right?" Fish said, proud of himself for knowing *something* about their world.

"That's right, but I didn't know that," she added. While she spoke, she took the slices of cheese and laid them atop the bread, which was still heating on the stove. "They were happy to take me," Nora continued, "since boats are always in need of boys to do the menial jobs: mending ropes, patching the hull, swabbing the decks. But they weren't too pleased when they learned that I was a girl."

"How did they discover it?"

Stabbing the toasted, cheese-covered slices with her knife, Nora lifted them off the stove and placed them on the plank. She shook her head. "The blasted seat of easement. I couldn't . . . you know . . . go in front of the other men."

Daniel had pointed out a few important parts and sections of the boat. Among them was a pair of platforms at the bow with a few head-sized circles cut through each. Daniel didn't need to explain what they were for; Fish saw two men squatting over the circles and deduced their function.

"Have you cleaned them yet?"

"No."

"You will," Nora said. "It's a gruesome task, truly foul, and it's left to the boys on the ship. That would be yourself, Daniel, and Nate. You'll be scrubbing the seats soon enough."

The thought of it made him cringe. "So what happened when they discovered you?"

"On any other boat, I might have been tossed over the side, since most pirates believe it's bad luck to have women on board. But Melinda was already here, so that wasn't their concern. As it happens, the regular cook was dying from a knife wound, and one of the men suggested that I be allowed to stay if I was effective in the galley. I was thrown down here and put to the test. I mixed up some gruel with hardtack, the men declared it the best they'd ever tasted, and Cobb gave me a position."

Fish peered at the greenish-gray substance in the cauldron. "This saved your life?"

"The standard was not very high, I admit," she said, hurriedly piling the salami and pickled vegetables on one of the cheese-covered slices of bread and folding the other on top. "But wait until you try this. It's my very own creation and I call it the sandwich, after my birthplace in England."

Still ravenous, Fish bit down and ripped a chunk out of the corner. It was salty, sweet, crunchy, chewy — a mix of flavors and textures the likes of which he'd never experienced. It felt as though he'd stuffed four different meals into his mouth at once. He took another bite, saw her watching him, and tried to smile to signal his approval, but his mouth was too packed.

"At first I was angry, being trapped in here when I wanted to be a real pirate, but it's better than patching the hull or scrubbing the deck. I've grown to like cooking, particularly when we stock up in the islands."

He attempted to respond, but his mouth was too full of cheese and meat and bread.

"The captain and his wife have watched over me, too," she said, proud of the added attention. "I'll tell you one thing: Melinda is not your average pirate's bride. He does what she tells him, I've heard."

Nora began picking up the food, packing everything away. "Now, be honest with me. How's the sandwich?"

One glance at Fish's hands would have been answer enough. The sandwich was gone, every last crumb and morsel. He spied a bit of melted cheese on the tip of one of his nails and nibbled it off. Then he said, honestly, "The best food I've ever had!"

Her face alight, Nora thanked him, then pointed to the partially eaten biscuit in his bowl of gruel. Out of a small hole in the center, a tiny green creature was wriggling its way out.

"Are you going to eat your worm?"

How to Break Up
a Sleep-Duel

Three weeks passed. They sailed into open ocean, and the heaving and swaying of the wave-rocked boat forced him to fall more than once. The food was terrible, the drinking water foul, and he was sick for nearly seven days. But Fish began to adjust to his new life. He lost all sense of time. When he finally asked one of the men what day it was, he realized that he'd missed his birthday. He had turned twelve without even knowing it.

Just before dawn each morning, he awoke to the rooster-like call of Moravius, which stirred the sailors as if they'd been splashed in the face with buckets of frigid seawater. The pirates would swing out of their hammocks, fold and hook them to the ceiling, stretch and growl, belch and cough, rub their eyes and faces vigorously, then stomp up to the deck. Fish always raced up before the other men, lowered a bucket into the sea, and rinsed his hands, face, hair, and feet with the cool water.

The men would gather on the deck, arrange themselves in rows, each one an arm's length from the next, and follow the actions and directions of a very energetic pirate known as Jumping Jack. He was all muscle and bald but for a ring of brown hair that made him look like a monk — Fish had seen him with Scab quite a few times. All the leaning this way, stretching that way, and the running and jumping in place were strange to Fish, but the other men followed Jumping Jack's every move, so he did the same.

After about ten minutes, they would finish with an odd little routine that involved leaping in the air, spreading your feet wide, and joining your hands together above your head as you landed, then reversing the action. The men called it a Jumping Jack; Fish found it very effective for shaking the sleep out of his head.

Next came the work. Sadly, Nora was right: Fish did have to wash the seats of easement — he alternated with Nate and Daniel. But the vast majority of his time was devoted to swabbing the decks. All through the day, he gripped the handle, pressing the head back and forth upon the wood. Standing all day was exhausting enough, but the work also made the smooth skin of his palms and fingers red and raw; Nora would lend him rags and old clothes to wrap around his hands, but these hardly helped.

He despised the swab for the pain it caused, but it also earned him respect. Fish performed feats with it that few men aboard the *Scurvy Mistress* thought possible. In the cabin, he scrubbed away the grime and slime, revealing handsome, richly grained wood. Men would come down to grab a few lengths of line or some other supplies, smack him on the back, and bellow, "Well done, boy! She'll be a new ship when you're finished!"

A potbellied pirate named Noah popped down one morning in search of a new box of nails and became completely disoriented. Noah was staring down at his feet as he walked, humming a tune, when he stopped and said, "Where am I?

What ship is this?" The floor was so clean that he failed to recognize it.

Daniel said the trip across the ocean would take six weeks or more. This sounded like an eternity at first, but the days raced by. Fish sometimes became so lost in his work that the chimes for mealtime, rung six hours apart, would often sound after what felt like a few minutes.

The crew's labors ceased not long after dark. To help educate Fish about their peculiar world, Cobb had given him a book, *Guidelines for the Enterprising Pirate*. Fish read it when he could, but generally he was too tired. He usually collapsed at the end of each day, exhausted from being on his knees, pushing the swab back and forth. Yet sleep never came quickly. It wasn't the lack of a proper bed; he could have slept on a pile of fieldstones. No, it was the noise that kept him awake. Late into the night the men would laugh and drink and sing in loud, rumbling voices, rarely in unison. For the most part they were terrible singers and sounded like they were part bullfrog, part dog. The only one among them who had any talent was Noah.

He was officially the ship's carpenter, which meant he was perpetually fixing cracks and leaks and splits in the aging wooden vessel. Noah always had a pencil tucked behind one ear and a nail or two behind the other. His face was round and flat, as if he'd been punched there too many times, and his hair was long, full, and greasy — he often wore it in a ponytail. Cobb gave him his name because he believed that Noah's skills matched those of the Bible's famed boatbuilder. But Noah was also the chief entertainer on the *Scurvy Mistress*.

Daniel said he could write a song in under ten seconds. He had ditties for every occasion, and Fish noticed that the men knew them well. Whenever a fight erupted, for example, they'd sing:

> *Well here we go with another row,*
> *Two pirates fighting each other.*
> *This one's fierce with his fists for sure,*
> *But that one hits like my mother.*

And the fights were nearly constant after dinner. Fish tried to intervene on several occasions, suggesting that the combatants might be better off discussing their disagreement, but he would invariably find himself flicked out of the scrum like an insignificant gnat. One night not too long into the trip, Daniel convinced him to abandon these attempts. "You can't reason with rum," he said.

Eventually the men would unfurl their hammocks, climb inside, and sleep. Fish didn't deserve a hammock — according to Scab — so he slept on some ragged bits of old sailcloth in one corner of the main cabin and used a not particularly putrocious head of cabbage wrapped in an old towel for a pillow. Some of the pirates slept like stones, moving not at all through the whole of the night, while others constantly turned and even screamed. Thimble sometimes shrieked like a frightened young girl. There were stretches of silence, too, but at these times Fish would hear the whisperlike footsteps of mice as they crept out in search of food. Once he watched a mouse crawl up and onto Scab's thick beard, where it nibbled at the crumbs left there from dinner. Scab woke up, saw the tiny rodent, thanked it, and fell back asleep.

Many of the men were sleepwalkers, too. Fish was no stranger to the phenomenon: His brother Conor was a particularly skilled sleep-*worker*. On more than one occasion the family would awake in the morning and find him lying flat in the field, his hands dirty from working the soil as he dreamed. Yet Fish had never seen two people sleepwalking in the same room, and on the *Scurvy Mistress* that became a common sight. Noah and Sammy the Stomach twice walked into each other, smacking their massive bellies together without waking. One night he watched Thimble and Jumping Jack move around each other as if they were dancing. Some of the Scalawags for Sausage would line up at the kitchen counter, their hands bearing imaginary bowls, waiting in their sleep for food that never arrived. Fish never interrupted these nocturnal wanderings until one strange night when he felt obliged.

The men were all sleeping quietly save for the occasional girlish shriek from Thimble, yet Fish couldn't drift off, regardless of how many times he adjusted his cabbage pillow. Since there were few moments of peace aboard the crowded ship, he ventured up to the deck for a quiet communion with the night sky.

Outside, Bat, who earned his name because he slept during the day and worked all through the night, manned the tiller, which was used to steer the ship. Owl, a pirate with sharp eyes, sat at his usual place atop the mast, scanning the dark horizon. The moon was bright. A bluish-white light fell over everything.

The scene was so calm, so peaceful, that Fish considered sleeping right there on deck until he heard a sudden clank of steel on steel. Snapped out of his reverie, he spun around and saw Daniel and Nate staring glassy-eyed at each other, their cutlasses drawn. This couldn't be. As far as he knew, they were friends, not foes.

This was a fight he had to stop. He charged forward, ready to jump between them, then stopped. The two boys' eyes were barely open. They were hardly even looking at each other, and they moved drowsily, as if they were struggling just to remain on their feet. The boys were sleep-fighting!

"Stand back, dragon," Daniel mumbled. "You'll not breathe your deadly fire on Daniel the Dragon Slayer."

"I'll save thee, Princess Nora my love," Nate returned, his voice nearly as sleepy and lifeless. "Nate the Great is here."

Nate had to be referring to the cook; given the way he'd looked at her before walking the plank, this was no surprise. But there would be no royal romance if Fish didn't stop these boys from cutting each other. At the same time, he couldn't simply jump between two boys brandishing cutlasses, even if they were half in dreamland.

He called up to Owl for help.

"I can't leave my post."

He yelled to Bat.

"Let them fight," the nocturnal pirate replied.

He had to stop it himself, but how? He spotted a bucket of wash water someone had forgotten to empty. That would do. He picked it up, ran toward the boys, then hit Nate and

Daniel with a torrent of murky, ice-cold water. The boys awoke, staring at each other and the weapons in their hands. Both were confused and neither sheathed his cutlass.

"Stop!" Fish yelled. "You were sleep-fighting!"

Nate turned to him, lowered his blade. "Sleep-fighting?"

"There is no such thing," Daniel said.

"He's right," Owl yelled down from above. "One of you would be bleeding if your boy there hadn't stepped in."

Daniel edged the tip of his weapon toward his belt. "I will if you will. . . ."

Nate agreed. The fight was over.

Daniel placed his hand on Fish's shoulder. "Thank you," he said.

"Yes," Nate added. "Thank you for saving my life . . . for the second time." He avoided Fish's eyes, first staring out at the ocean, then down at the deck. "I should have said something earlier . . . but I was too . . ."

Fish thought of a few fitting words, but Daniel offered one first. "Stubborn?"

Nate kicked at the deck with his right foot. "Yes, but I thank you now sincerely."

"It was nothing," Fish replied.

"No," Nate said. "It most certainly was not. I am indebted to you. Although I do have one small request."

"Yes?"

Nate wiped his face, then wrung out the bottom of his soaked shirt. "Before you rescue me next, would you consider a method that is not quite so wet?"

Marriage Counseling

The very next morning, Fish was sitting at breakfast with the Over and Unders, learning about the intricacies of obscure knots, when Scab bellowed his name. Fish held up his hands instinctively, expecting to be hit. But Scab demanded to know what Fish had been doing up on deck the previous night.

"Stopping Daniel and Nate from cutting each other," he said proudly.

"Did I allow you up there in the first place?"

"I couldn't sleep."

"Then I suppose we are not working you hard enough. From now on, you will be on night duty, in addition to your labors during the day. There is always scrubbing to do."

Noah, who was eating nearby, pulled out a pencil and said, "That would make a nice chorus." Then he coughed and intoned:

> *Sailing across the ocean blue*
> *There's always scrubbing to do.*

Not one for singing, Scab raised his hand at the songwriter, who flinched, fumbling with the pencil behind his ear, and promptly turned back to his breakfast.

Before stomping off, Scab jabbed his cutlass at the rim of Fish's bowl, spilling his last few mouthfuls of gruel onto the deck. "Clean that up, too," he growled.

That night after dinner, Bat, who had just woken up, approached Fish. "Good morning!" he said. "Time for work."

The deck was wet and cold, the work not nearly as satisfying. Fish liked to see the results of his labors, but it was too dark; he was scrubbing blind. After about an hour, he decided it might be a good idea to lie down and rest his head on a coil of rope. Just for a moment. When he woke up, he would scrub with renewed fervor. His eyes were beginning to give in to the fatigue when he heard a curse. A woman's voice.

"That man!" she shouted. "That man will put me in my grave!"

Fish grabbed his swab and walked back toward the cabin. He found Melinda pacing and mumbling to herself.

"What man?" he asked. "Are you not well?"

Melinda stopped and glared at Fish as if he'd woken her from a dream. She didn't answer him, but Fish could tell when someone needed to talk. His mother used to have such moments. There was a look she had, as if there were a thunderstorm in her head and she didn't know whether to endure it or let it loose. His father, brothers, and sisters would avoid her at such times, but Fish would shadow his mother, asking questions. Often she'd stomp off and request that she be left alone, but occasionally a flood of words would rush from her mouth. He rarely understood what she was talking about, but in the end she'd usually smile and kiss him on the forehead, so he knew he'd done well. What he learned from these rants was that his mother sometimes needed someone to listen to her.

"No," she answered after a pause, "I'm not well. But why should you care?"

Her long red hair was pulled back, her full face alive with frustration. This was the first time he'd been alone with her since the day of the raid, when he'd tricked her in the cabin. He hoped she had forgiven him. "Are you still angry with me because of the —?"

"Of course I'm angry! Have you any notion of just how shameful it is to be tricked by a messenger boy? My husband would have me stashed away in our cabin day and night for my safety, but I have worked — no, slaved — to prove to him that a woman like myself is thoroughly capable of living amidst scoundrels. And being duped by a boy has not helped. Your antics set me back a good four years!" She pulled out a pistol. "He's making me carry this with me all the time now, and I abhor guns!"

"But why a gun? I didn't threaten you. In fact, I found . . . find you very intimidating."

She put away the pistol, crossed her arms on her chest, then tilted her chin. "Because of my somewhat ample figure?" she asked.

"No, no! I don't mean that. I . . ."

Thankfully, Melinda laughed. "The little gentleman! So afraid to insult a lady! Well, don't worry yourself, Fish, I am hardly offended. I am proudly a woman of some weight. And your fears are justifiable. I'm certain I could toss you across this deck as if you truly were a fish."

"Undoubtedly," he said, uncertain whether to laugh, too.

"And the captain? You fear him, too, I imagine."

No, that wasn't quite true. Fish feared Scab. And Moravius, too, because of his size. But not Captain Cobb. "I respect him," he said. Cobb was a powerful man, but Fish could tell that he wasn't prone to violence. "He is more controlled than the other men," he continued. "Whenever he appears poised to pop, he traces that scar on his chin and settles himself."

"You noticed that? How observant!"

"Why does he do that?" Fish asked.

"A reminder. He has a temper, believe me. And he could not control it so well in his youth. Long before I met him, he engaged in a duel with a man who'd once been a good friend. His friend left him with that scar, but our Captain Cobb took the man's life. The death still haunts him, and that scar reminds him that violence often leads to undesirable ends."

They were silent for a moment, and then Melinda's mood changed. "We've drifted," she said, and she wasn't speaking of the boat. "I believe we were talking about how you betrayed me, correct?"

Reluctantly, Fish nodded.

"It's not merely that you duped me. You may have done

the one thing worse than overpowering me. You tricked me by drawing out my maternal instincts! I'm supposed to stifle those urges. I'm a member of a pirate crew, after all."

"I was wrong," Fish said. "And I am sorry. But I should return to my duties. . . ."

He turned and stepped toward the bow.

"No, no," she called. "Come back. I accept your apology. And you are not the reason I was upset, anyway." The cabin door opened behind her. Fish saw someone emerge, but Melinda was looking away and failed to notice. "I'm angry because the leader of our enterprising band can be such a selfish, pompous, arrogant, ignorant —"

"Fool?" Cobb asked, standing with his mostly bald, wigless head gleaming in the moonlight. "Or would you prefer to call me an imbecile? Tell me, Melinda, what choice names had you planned next?"

Even in the darkness, Fish could see her round face redden. " 'Imbecile' is perfect, actually."

"And you are a mule! A stubborn mule!"

This was unfortunate. Fish wanted nothing to do with this argument. If only she would let him resume his scrubbing. He picked up his swab and slowly started to edge away.

Cobb began speaking in a near whisper. "How could you call me selfish?" he asked. "How many times must I tell you that I'm doing this for us? This treasure will allow us to live the life you've always wanted."

Now he sounded like a husband, Fish thought, and not a pirate.

"That doesn't mean you can treat me like one of your crew until we find it!" Melinda shouted back. "Mind your behavior. Be a gentleman, like young Fish here."

"A gentleman! Easy for him, a boy, who doesn't have an entire crew of men counting on him to lead them to riches. Or perhaps he'd like to assume control of the ship, too, now that he's taken control of my marriage? Perhaps he could solve our grand conundrum in the cabin?"

But Fish was not ready to solve anything. In fact, he was utterly lost. He'd been reduced to a pawn and, for the first time in weeks, he felt like jumping over the side, just to get away from them. An hour sniffing Foot's yellowing toes or inhaling Scab's ripe, nasty breath would have been preferable to another minute stuck between these two.

"I bet he could," Melinda countered.

"Fine," Cobb answered. "Bring him in."

The captain, fuming, returned to the cabin. Melinda looked at the door, then at Fish, who was thoroughly confused. What had they agreed to?

"I am sorry, but you have to go inside. I know him. His mind is set."

"On what?" Fish asked. "What is the grand conundrum?"

"You will find out in a moment. Though I doubt he truly expects you to solve our puzzle." She placed a hand on his head. "But would you grant me a favor?"

Fish agreed, unsure of how else to respond.

"Prove him wrong."

SECRETS IN THE COINS

Cobb was standing over the table in the center of the cabin. The coins from the stolen purse were spread across the surface, and he laid his hand on Fish's back. "So?"

So? How was he supposed to know what to do? Cobb acted as if Fish could simply look at the coins and solve their problem. Melinda was watching him expectantly, too. Even the giant appeared interested. But Fish had no idea what they were looking for.

He stared at the different coins. Some were gold, others silver, still others the color of rust. The discs varied in thickness and size, too. A few were no larger than his thumbnail, while most were three or four times as large. Some were chipped at the edges, irregular. But what any of this meant he did not know. Unsure of how else to proceed, he started to count.

There were forty-one in all. The gold coins, he noticed, had a glow that suggested they'd been recently polished. He moved these, twelve in all, to one side of the table, then slid the remaining twenty-nine to the opposite side.

"Could I have a hint?" Fish asked at last.

"We believe that the secret to the location of the treasure is disguised in this mix of coins," Melinda said.

"We don't believe it," Cobb said. "We *know* it."

"What treasure?" Fish asked.

"*The* treasure!" Melinda said. "It will be one of the greatest discoveries in the history of our trade. And we will find it" — she directed this statement at Cobb, as if trying to encourage him — "but at present we find ourselves mired."

Thoughts of gold and jewels and glimmering stones flashed in Fish's head. And horses! A whole herd of them! "What sort of treasure?"

"That's not for you to know — yet," Cobb answered. "In fact, when you leave, you may not inform the men, not a single one of them, what you were doing in here tonight."

That would be easy; Fish barely knew himself. "So how is the location hidden in the coins?"

"We are not certain. They could be a map, or clues of some sort."

A map? How could a collection of coins be a map? Maps were drawn out on paper. They were supposed to be clear and detailed.

Melinda stood next to him. "We noticed that these —"

"Melinda! Let the boy come to his own conclusions."

"Or we can inform him of our suspicions and move forward from there," she said, ignoring her husband's request. "Now, Fish, as I was saying, you'll notice that these coins" — she pointed to the golden pile — "are all the same shape and size, and bear the same likeness."

Melinda grouped them so each was lying flat, then flipped five of them so that all twelve were faceup, revealing the same small bust of a regal-looking woman — a queen. "This suggests they were all minted from the same mold. They are almost exactly alike."

He stuck on the word "almost."

"But?"

"But for one detail," she answered, and then flipped each of the coins so the queen's profile was facing down.

The opposite sides of the coins were covered with images of what he guessed were vines and leaves. They appeared to be identical.

He leaned in to study one coin closely and spied amidst those tangles a tiny letter. He eyed a neighboring coin. A different letter, but in the same spot. Quickly he surveyed the rest.

Melinda noted his progress. "As you see, each has a single letter" — she pointed to a small *E* on one of the coins — "except for one, which has two letters, an *E* and an *N*."

Fish felt Cobb press against his shoulder. The captain, apparently abandoning the contest with his wife, could not resist joining them. "I believe —"

The giant coughed. Cobb looked up at him. "*We* believe that if we were to arrange these coins in the proper order, there could be a message. But we have not yet discovered anything sensible."

"We think it's an anagram," Melinda explained.

"The goal is to take all of the letters — *R, R, D, E, Z, B, S, A, G, A, E, N, E* — and rearrange them to form words," Cobb said.

As Fish watched, the captain shuffled the coins until the letters, lined up, spelled *BRAZENED RAGES*. He slid them around a few more times, producing new arrangements of words — *GREEN ZEBRAS AD, ZARBENS AGREED* — but nothing that could be construed as a sensible message.

"We have considered several solutions, as you see, but have found no clear answers. Certainly pirates and explorers are often brazen folk, and susceptible to rage, but 'brazened rages' blows us in no obvious direction. Naturally we assumed that 'Zarbens' in 'Zarbens agreed' would be a person, yet in our many volumes we can find no record of a man —"

"Nor a woman," Melinda cut in.

Impatiently, Cobb continued: "— nor a woman with that name, so 'Zarbens agreed' is not our answer, either. 'Zebras' suggests we might find what we're looking for somewhere on the vast continent of Africa, but why 'green'? And why 'AD'? Unfortunately," Cobb added quietly, "we are no closer to our answer than when we first spied this collection."

Fish picked up one of the coins, turned it over, and studied the woman's face. She certainly was regal. And obviously royal: She wore a crown and a massive necklace. Then he examined the opposite side again and noticed something else. "A fish!"

"Yes," Melinda noted, "all of the coins in that group feature that same small fish. What we're looking for, though, are the differences, not the similarities. Elements unique to each coin that might suggest some sort of larger pattern or code."

Cobb pulled on the tip of his long nose. "The letters . . . do you notice any words?"

No, he did not. He probably knew half as many words as the captain and his wife. If they'd been studying these coins for weeks and still hadn't discovered any hidden phrases, he doubted that he'd be the one to find them. So, instead, he turned his attention elsewhere. "What about these?" Fish asked, pointing to the other pile.

Once more Moravius coughed, as if he were trying to say something.

"Decoys," Cobb said. "Obviously mixed in with the others to mislead us."

Perhaps he was correct, but Fish was drawn to them nonetheless. Each of the coins in the mismatched pile was different in color and shape from the next, and in the pictures or icons on their faces, too. "So, if the other coins, based on their similarities, were minted in the same place, then these might have been forged in different places, right?"

"Yes. Which is yet another reason for us to ignore them," Cobb said. "A single man compiled this collection. Only he knew where the great treasure was hidden, and he spread clues to its location across the world. We know that he embedded hints in these coins. But why go to the trouble of creating twenty-nine distinct coins?"

"That would be far too laborious," Melinda added.

"Yet forging a dozen, each with a unique letter in the same spot on each disc, would be comparatively simple." Cobb stood back from the table, tapped it with his fist. "The gold coins, young man. The gold coins hold our clue."

Fish understood their reasoning, but he couldn't ignore the allure of the others. He held one up and scratched at the grime with his thumbnail.

Cobb sighed with frustration, but Melinda asked for his patience. "Let's see what Fish finds."

Fish picked up another coin and cleaned its surface, too. With the grime stripped away, he noticed a link between the pair.

One of the coins was the size of his thumbnail, the other twice as large. But each bore the same small icon of a bird. Nearly everything else about them was different. The profiles on their faces were nothing alike. On the opposite sides, one featured a scene of a storm-tossed sea, the other a castle wall. Yet they shared that one detail. The bird had to mean something.

Melinda leaned in closely, studied what he'd uncovered.

Moravius stepped over, too. "Aha!" he said. "How simple!"

Fish jumped back from the table. The giant could speak after all!

"Moravius! Silence!" Cobb yelled.

The giant slapped one of his enormous palms over his mouth.

"It's too late now, Walter," Melinda said. "The boy heard him."

Cobb huffed. Moravius watched him expectantly.

"Oh, Walter, would you allow him to talk?"

"How many times must I tell you? A savage, mute giant is much more frightening than a supremely intelligent one! And you . . . you are using my given name. You are not supposed to —"

"Calm yourself, Walter. When we are in the privacy of our own cabin, I am not going to call you Captain Cobb. Furthermore, I think it is insulting to Moravius to force him to remain mute even in here. He is more intelligent than you and I combined, after all."

"Fine," Cobb said. "Moravius, you are free to speak."

The giant paused as if holding his breath. He was obviously unsure of what to do next. With one of his huge, pawlike hands he rubbed his bearded neck and crooked nose, then made a few clucking noises in his throat.

"Th-thank you, Wa-walter," Moravius began.

A great grumbling sounded in his chest. He freed something large and very unpleasant from deep in his throat. Fish watched him remove a beautiful purple silk handkerchief from a pocket of his grimy coat, deftly flip it open, and wipe his mouth. "This is quite an honor, though of course I understand if you wish for me to remain silent outside the cabin. Your silent-giant-makes-a-scary-giant assumption is in all likelihood a fair one. If anyone on board knew I was an accomplished scholar at Cambridge, I'm not sure I'd have quite the same sway as I do now. Yet one cannot help but wonder —"

"Moravius?"

"Yes, Walter?"

"I did not ask for a monologue."

"Ah, yes, of course. I apologize. I haven't spoken in so long. Like a ship with neither sails nor tiller, caught in a current, my thoughts are afloat on —"

"Moravius," Cobb interrupted, "if you keep carrying on like this I will order you to be silent again."

"Understood. But one more question?"

After a pause Cobb reluctantly replied, "Yes?"

"May I have a shave? My poor skin hasn't felt a fresh breeze in years, and I believe —"

"Absolutely not!" Cobb said. "The beard is essential to your brutish appearance."

Moravius appealed to Melinda. "I'm sorry, Moravius," she said. "But I think Walter is right."

Fish agreed — the rough, tangled beard gave the giant the look of an untamed animal.

"And that?" Moravius said, pointing to the wig on Cobb's desk. "I suppose that glorified mat is essential to *your* image: the educated rogue?"

Cobb picked up his wig and placed it on his head. "Yes, that is exactly my —"

"Oh, do take it off, Walter," Melinda cut in. "It looks like a dead animal sleeping on your head."

"Or the end of a swab," Fish added.

Melinda and Moravius laughed uproariously in response, but Cobb did not. Next time, Fish would think before speaking.

"This brand of wig is very fashionable in London!" Cobb said to his wife. He removed the wig and held it out. "This dead animal, as you call it, is a reminder to the crew that I am not merely another seagoing scoundrel. I am a gentleman, a man of nobility. My father was a hero of the war and I was once an officer of the British navy. I was educated at Cambridge!"

Melinda motioned to Moravius. "But you finished far below the savage here."

At this, both Moravius and Melinda resumed chuckling. Cobb's face and large ears turned purple, and Fish worried that he was going to reach for his cutlass or one of the many pistols lying throughout the cabin. Instead, though, he began to laugh along with them. Fish joined in, too, although he was not quite sure what was so funny.

After a moment, Moravius encouraged Fish to continue.

Fish searched the rest of the pile, scratching at the grime and polishing the coins as best he could. Though varied in almost every way, each of the coins in that pile of twenty-nine were linked to at least one other through a small figure like that bird. He picked out a knife, a snake, a lion, and more. These figures weren't always easy to find, as they were often hidden within a larger scene on the face of the coin, but they were there.

Cobb, watching Fish work, praised every tiny discovery. This was far better than being complimented on his well-scrubbed floors. He glanced over at Melinda. She smiled, then pitched her head forward as if to say, "Don't stop now!"

At one point Moravius and Fish reached out for the same coin, but the giant quickly removed his sausagelike fingers, allowing the boy to proceed on his own.

The work proved to be fairly fast. In just a few minutes, he had sorted the grimy, mismatched coins into nine stacks, with anywhere from two to seven coins in each: twenty-nine apparently mismatched discs sorted into nine piles. One stack included the coins with the figure of a snake, the next was comprised of those with a knife, then a flower, and so on. Fish arranged the stacks in a row ascending from shortest to tallest.

"What about the golden coins?" Cobb asked.

Fish had pushed them to the side; he didn't think they were relevant. "They don't have any of the same figures as the coins in this group," he said.

"What if we were wrong all along?" Moravius asked. "What if the golden coins are the decoys?"

"The letters could be random," Melinda added. "Those coins could have been tossed into the purse merely to confuse would-be treasure hunters."

"Yes," Cobb added quietly, immersed in thought, "that could be. . . ."

Fish stared at the stacks and felt a powerful urge to continue rearranging them, as if he might solve the puzzle through action alone. But he had not an inkling about how to proceed next.

Thankfully, though, he noticed that Cobb, Melinda, and Moravius were just as puzzled. The captain moved back to the other side of the small room and sat on the edge of his desk, smoking his pipe, eyeing the coins with deep concentration.

Moravius remained next to Fish, bent over the table. "Perhaps the piles should be . . ." he began, then let his words trail off.

Melinda, too, muttered a kind of half thought. "Or if we were to consider . . ."

They sat like this, alternately quiet and mumbling, for some time. Fish resisted the urge to continue arranging the coins to see if he could find another clue. Before long, though, the lull in the action and conversation began to produce a lull in his mind. The boat swayed leisurely as it sailed up and down the ocean's long, smooth waves, rocking everyone inside. The excitement of his initial discovery faded. Weariness began to seep once more through his muscles and bones.

THE ART OF NOT-FIGHTING

Fish was sleeping heavily, deep in a dream in which he was underwater, pulling potatoes out of the sandy ocean floor, when he awoke to a fierce explosion of pain in his ribs. Another one followed, in his ankle. It felt like he was being struck by a hammer. Fearing a third blow, he scampered into a crouch and held up his hands. Eyes still crusted with sleep, wondering what happened to those underwater potatoes, he begged, "Stop! Please!"

"Mercy? In exchange for your blatant disregard of the rules and schedule of the ship, not to mention my very own orders?"

Scab. The stinking pirate was standing before him with Thimble at his side. He had all the rage of a bonfire in his eyes, yet red-faced, well-dressed Thimble was definitely the one who had kicked him. Fish had heard that he wore wooden-toed boots. Now he'd have the bruises to prove it.

Overhead he heard the stomping of feet. The men were performing their exercises, which meant he must have overslept. "I didn't hear the call. . . ."

"And last night? I ordered you to clean the decks and instead you spent the evening relaxing in the captain's quarters? Thimble, how many evenings have you spent in our distinguished captain's cabin?"

The wiry tailor held out both hands as if he were ready to count up the number on his fingers. Then, with mock astonishment, he answered, "Why, none!"

Fish tried to interject. "But the captain ordered —"

Scab ignored him. "An able seaman, an accomplished and experienced pirate with a noted thirst, and you have never once reclined in the captain's cabin over a bottle of his fine wine?"

"Not once!" Thimble answered. "He won't even let me mend his clothes. He has that woman do it instead, a fact that I find to be positively —"

"Enough!" Scab barked. "We are not down here to complain about what Cobb thinks of your needlework! We are here to determine why it is that young Fish here has enjoyed a privilege that has not been extended to the rest of us. You must be a grand brand of pirate, Fish, to be invited inside after only four weeks aboard the ship."

If they would only give him a moment to explain himself. "Ask the captain; he will —"

Thimble resumed as though Fish were not even there. "To be a great pirate, he must be a skilled sailor."

"And an accomplished fighter, too," Scab added. "Yet I don't recall ever seeing him brandish a blade."

"Nor I."

"I must say that I should love to see this prodigy in action."

"I don't fight," Fish said, his voice fired by frustration. "I don't even know how to hold a sword."

"Not a concern," Scab answered. "You can use your fists instead."

With that, he grabbed Fish by the back of his too-large shirt and hauled him clear off the floor, then tossed him against the stairs. His ribs screamed with pain.

"Up!" Thimble yelled, kicking him sharply in the leg.

Stumbling, Fish half crawled, half climbed onto the deck. The men had just finished their exercises and were awaiting Scab's call to begin the day's work. Instead, he announced a demonstration. "For your morning entertainment, our newest crew member would like to display the swiftness of his fists."

Fish held up his hands, palms out, hoping to clarify once again the fact that he was not interested in fighting, but the crew had already begun stomping and shouting. Their appetites for action primed, there would be no calming them now.

"How about . . ." Scab scanned the deck and then said, "Young Nate!"

Nate stepped out of the crowd. "Sir, I would rather not —"

"Nonsense. Do you want to be a boarder or not?"

Nate stammered, unsure of how to respond. He stared at Fish. They were friends now; he'd even been helping Fish with his work. He had shown him a trick for cleaning the seats of easement in half the time and secured him a hat to keep the sun out of his eyes on particularly bright days.

"This is an order," Scab shouted. "You are to engage your young friend — your savior — in combat. Despite your lamentable past failures, you are a pirate, are you not?"

This question, a clear challenge, emboldened Nate. The reluctance drained from his face and posture. "I am," he said sternly.

"And you won't deny your brothers the entertainment of a small scuffle, will you?"

Fish stiffened as he saw that Nate was eyeing him now, not Scab. He hoped the boy would refuse, but this was unlikely at best. They were friends, but they were also lowly boys aboard a pirate ship, and they had been ordered to fight. Nate shrugged, raised his fists, and began moving toward him.

The men whooped louder and formed a ring around the boys. Nate circled, moving slowly, as if waiting for the right moment to strike. He obviously wasn't deriving any joy from the situation, but it didn't look as if he intended to hold back, either. He rolled up his sleeves, revealing unusually large forearms for a boy his age. If he hits me, Fish thought, it's going to hurt.

At first, Fish mirrored Nate's movements. He wasn't sure what else to do. Nate jumped closer, then backed away. The men cheered. There was no place to hide, nothing to stand between them. Yet Fish did not want to run. He did not want to fight, either, but he refused to run. They continued moving around each other. He saw Cobb, Moravius, and Melinda watching from the quarterdeck, above the captain's cabin. They weren't going to intervene. He could see that. But would they be disappointed if he didn't fight?

Nate lunged in and wrapped his arm around Fish's head. "What are you doing?" he whispered. "Hit me a few times, I will do the same, and it will all be over. We have to give them a show."

Nate released him and Fish glanced up again at the quarterdeck. The captain gestured encouragingly, urging him to fight. Instead of spurring him to strike, though, it convinced him to stop. He was no fighter. And he never intended to become one, whether he lived among pirates or not. So he stopped, folded his hands behind his back, and proclaimed, "I refuse to fight."

Nate lowered his fists. "Fish, you can't refuse!"

Fish remained motionless with his hands behind his back. The cheers faded. The men were confused. This was not supposed to happen.

Noah began to sing:

> *When Nate the Great lifted up his fists*
> *And circled 'round the deck,*
> *The clean-scrubbing Fish simply stayed in place*
> *A frozen, nervous wreck.*

"I'm not nervous!" Fish shouted over the ensuing laughs. "I said that I refuse to fight."

"But you are a pirate; you have to fight!" Nate said, pleading with him.

"Hit him anyway," Scab ordered.

Nate took two steps toward him and fired his fist like a shot from a pistol. A very brief flash of pain erupted near Fish's left eyebrow, and then darkness enveloped him.

Fish awoke near the galley, lying on a pile of sailcloth. Someone was holding a bottle of rum beneath his nose, and the fumes from the powerful alcohol were rushing directly to his head. His vision was blurred, and he started to rub his eyes with the backs of his hands when he felt another shot of intense pain.

"Careful," said Daniel. "You have a nice lump there."

"I am sorry for that," said Nate. "But you should have ducked."

Fish pushed away the bottle. He squinted; Nora was there with them, too. He tried to sit up, but his head felt like it was being tossed in the waves.

His friends, however, offered little sympathy.

"*I refuse to fight?*" Nora said. "What were you thinking?"

Fish clutched his stomach, which was on the edge of revolt. The only positive outcome of his eye injury was that he no longer felt the pain in his ribs. He took a few breaths, collected himself. "I don't like fighting," he explained. "I don't think other people should fight, and I have absolutely no interest in doing so myself."

"But you are on a pirate ship!" Nora said. She pulled up one of her sleeves, revealing several of her hidden blades. "Even the cook has to learn how to fight!"

"Well," Fish said, sitting himself up, "I don't want to."

"But you don't understand . . ." Nate stammered, too perplexed by Fish's response to finish his sentence.

"Unless . . ." Daniel began.

"Unless what?" Fish asked.

"Unless we teach you how to not-fight."

Nora rolled her sleeve back down. *What?*

Daniel jumped to his feet. "Take out one of your knives and try to cut me."

"Why?"

"I'll show you."

Nora removed a small blade from her waistband and stabbed at Daniel's right shoulder. At the last instant, he rotated so Nora only struck air. "Now the head," he said, and when Nora sliced there, he ducked. "And the stomach," he added, starting to enjoy himself. Fish thought he might jump out of the way to avoid the blade, but instead he moved only his hips, twisting and shifting them to one side while keeping his feet in place. Again, Nora's strike missed its target. "You have to be fast," he said, dodging the fourth, unrequested stab, "but it's something you could learn. You can use your hands, too," he added as he avoided another one of Nora's strikes by turning his shoulders and pushing her blade hand at the same time.

"Impressive," Nate said.

"You can duck, dodge, block, and tire your opponent out. You have a lot to learn, but these maneuvers would be preferable to standing there with your chin out saying, 'I refuse.' All that will earn you is an early date with the ocean floor."

"It's a dangerous strategy," Nora said. "He will need to be good."

"Very good," Nate added.

Nora stopped, took a breath, and returned the blade to her belt. Though he doubted that she truly hoped to injure Daniel, Fish could tell she was annoyed that she had not been able to strike him at least once.

"I can teach you," Daniel offered.

Fish considered the plan. It wouldn't count as fighting, exactly, and he might be able to emerge from future stand-offs with less painful injuries.

He stood up; Nate, apparently remorseful, hurried to help him. Fish reached out to shake Daniel's hand and accept his offer, but Nora interrupted, walloping Fish's new instructor on the shoulder.

She was happy to see that Daniel failed to dodge it. "Yes, Fish will have to be good. Better than you."

THE CHAIN
OF CHUACAR

The excitement of crossing the Atlantic faded sometime during his fifth week on the ship. The thrill of being out on the open ocean, under the sun and the ceiling of bright white stars at night, should have lasted through the entire journey, but before long, the blue water became as familiar as the farm's green fields, the heavens no more interesting than the mist that settled over the cottage each night. His world was all wood and water now instead of fields and trees, but the peculiarities of the ship were no longer very peculiar. The gruel didn't taste as awful, and his stomach no longer protested the receipt of those rocklike lumps of hardtack. Cabbage, if properly positioned, could actually make a very nice pillow. Even his nose had trained itself to handle the new world: Scab once pressed Fish's face to one of Foot's rancid toes, and Fish inhaled without fainting or flinching. His hands adjusted, too; the raw, red skin had become tough and calloused.

There was one task, however, that he could not quite get accustomed to: scrubbing the seats of easement. The work was stinking and vile, and you could never really clean the seats completely. But, as Daniel explained, it was part of the life of a ship's boy, as much a constant as the rolling waves.

If these cleaning sessions were the low points, the regular not-fighting lessons with Daniel were one of the highlights of each day. Cobb called an end to Fish's night duty after only a week — which made Scab furious — so he used this time to train with his friend. Fish proved to be a fast learner; he enjoyed studying how to not-fight, seeing how nearly everything on board could be used in self-defense, including the mast, boom, tackle, barrels, and crates. His friend showed him how to use the handle of his swab, a spare line of rope, or even a belt to fend off the thrusts of a cutlass. Before long, he could dodge a punch and block a sword with ease.

The men were also acquiring a kind of respect for him. Not as an equal, exactly, but as a worthy member of the crew. They were especially appreciative of his cleaning skills. Sammy the Stomach requested that he devote extra care to the floor beneath his hammock, as he believed it made him sleep more peacefully, and Simon invented a new word for the slightly less vile state of the cabin. One evening while Fish was at work on a bloodstain that several of the men swore had been there for three years at least, Simon kneeled beside him, adjusted his spectacles, rubbed his tiny chin, and said, "No longer dirty, but not quite immaculate yet, either. Shall we call it dirtaculate?"

During meals, one of the groups would typically invite Fish over so they could impress upon him the importance of their particular concern. The Scalawags for Sausage lectured him on the subtleties of salted meat. The Tea Leaves explained the benefits of their chosen beverage in comparison to coffee and sang of the wonderful things their countrymen, the British, had supposedly done for his home island. The One-eyed

Willies waxed on about depth perception and demanded that he judge who among them had the finest eye patch.

The men imparted critical knowledge, too. The Over and Unders demonstrated the versatility of different tying techniques. Knot, their leader, acted bitterly toward him at first, as the boy had caused him some embarrassment by escaping that day he saved Nate. But the pirate warmed to him before too long. He taught Fish how to tie a range of knots, demonstrated which ones were suited for binding a prisoner's wrists or a package, and explained how to loosen them should he ever find himself captive on an enemy ship. Knot's favorite was the Slippery Noodle; he told Fish that most sailors believed that only a few people in the world could untie this maze of line, but with a bit of practice it proved to be rather easy. "The key is not to force a knot," he explained, "but to romance it, to convince it that it wants to be freed."

Sammy the Stomach, in addition to his unofficial role as chief eater, was also the main gunner. He introduced Fish to the ship's cannons. One evening during dinner, he pointed his biscuit at each of the guns on the larboard side, naming them in turn. "That's Meat Pie. She's a minion. Then we have Zucchini, another minion; Sausage One, she's a six; and Sausage Two, an eight —"

"An eight?" Fish asked.

"An eight fires an eight-pound shot, a six fires a six. Meat Pie got her name because she minces the decks of opposing ships. Zucchini, she looks like a zucchini. In shape, I mean, not color. As for the Sausage sisters, they earned such esteemed monikers because they don't impress on the outside, but inside they have power. On the starboard side we have Chocolate, Ham, Whiskey, and Mutton."

"Why Mutton?"

"I love mutton, so I had to name one of my guns after the stuff. She is a good girl: a six-pounder that sprays splinters as if she were a twelve."

Scab, Thimble, or one of their group would also summon him on occasion, but they usually launched a grog-sodden hunk of tack, or worse, at his head before he got too close.

He was mocked, taught, lectured, and appealed to, but he was privy to more casual banter as well, and it was during these conversations that Fish began to hear rumors that Cobb was searching for the famous Chain of Chuacar. According to the men, he had hunted for it in the past, in various parts of the world, with mixed success. He would uncover some gold or jewels — along with a new and tantalizing clue — but never the chain itself.

The stories about this treasure varied, and Fish wasn't sure who to believe, but he enjoyed Nora's version the best. She had a rare talent for storytelling. Her version of any tale, real or imagined, would always be two or three times longer than anyone else's rendition and far more enjoyable. And her green eyes were suited for the role of storyteller — peering into them, Fish felt a sensation of mystery and depth. He was dining at her counter one rainy evening when she told him what she knew of the chain.

"According to the legend," she began, "Chuacar, a mighty king, summoned one hundred of the finest craftsmen in the world to his palace following the death of his beloved wife. The king was so convinced he would never find another woman to match his lost queen that he declared the city itself to be his bride. This caused some confusion among his followers, who wondered how the king would marry an entire city. How would he talk to her? How would he look in her eyes? Did she even have eyes? If he wanted to stroke her hair, would he caress the branches of the great trees in the central square? Would people be allowed to walk through the city, or would the king complain that they were stomping all over his bride?

"His chief adviser, a young woman whose name has been lost to history, suggested that if he was going to make the city his queen, he would need to see to it that she was dressed like one. She told him it would be wise to repaint the city in bright new colors, to plant more flowers and, most importantly, to adorn it with jewels. The adviser told him that the new queen would need earrings, which could be hung from the leaves of the trees, and many large gold bracelets, which could be wrapped around the trunks. Finally, she said, the queen would need a beautiful necklace — the largest, most magnificent necklace in all the world. The king agreed, summoned his craftsmen, and ordered them to make a golden chain large enough to wrap around the whole of the city."

"The entire city?" Fish asked.

"The entire city," Nora replied.

"So what happened?"

"The craftsmen made the chain, but the adviser sailed off with it before the king had even seen it. Centuries passed, and then a lone explorer — Wentworth Collins — found the chain. But it was far too large for a single man to remove himself. He was forced to travel on, hoping that he'd be able to return one day with a crew. Years went by, yet Collins never gathered enough resources. He was so worried that someone would try to steal it from him that he never told anyone about the chain. But he did leave clues to its location in various ports and far-off places, and all manner of adventurers and treasure hunters have been searching for it ever since. Some say the king is still looking, too — as a ghost."

When she finished, Fish found himself smiling wide, like a small child. He was certain that this was the treasure Cobb, Melinda, and Moravius were so reluctant to tell him about, the one linked to the coins. He also knew that Scab would find the prospect of a treasure hunt appalling. He recalled the argument between Scab and Cobb the very first day he snuck aboard the *Scurvy Mistress*. Even then, Scab suspected that Cobb was searching for the chain.

Yet he wondered how the rest of the crew would feel about the quest. Fish soon learned that the Scalawags for Sausage were ambivalent; they were happy with the haul from the recent raid and far more concerned with the fine foods they would purchase when they came into port than any future adventures. But he heard Thimble telling the Tea Leaves that it would be "a tragedy, a travesty, a terrible travail." The One-eyed Willies generally preferred quests: Due to their incomplete eyesight, they weren't terribly useful in raids. Most of the men, though, really had no firm opinion, and as Nora explained, this was the sensible stance. Cobb had not even confirmed the rumors that he was seeking chain.

During one of their not-fighting sessions on deck a few nights after his talk with Nora, Fish asked Daniel for his opinion. Daniel related a version of the same story Fish had heard a few times, but he added that the chain was now guarded by fire-breathing dragons. This was doubtful; Daniel added a dragon to nearly every story he told.

Still, Daniel said he had faith in his captain and preferred quests to raids. "But fighting will always be a part of our life," he added, "so we have to train. Are you ready?"

Fish steadied himself and prepared to not-fight.

"Remember, you're not going to be striking anyone yourself, so your aim is to defeat your opponent by other means." Daniel swept his blade toward his legs, but Fish jumped, pulling up his knees and feet, causing Daniel to miss. "You must exhaust your opponent, force him to quit. These pirates, they're not as quick or as spry as you and I. Grog, rum, too many years at sea have slowed them. If you dodge enough, keep moving, force your foe to race around the boat, he will give up before too long. But if you want to end it more rapidly, you must disarm him."

The statement was sensible, but not entirely helpful. During their lessons, Daniel had repeatedly emphasized that Fish should never let the pirates get too close. "There is no dodging when one of those men has your neck in the crook of his elbow," he had said. So how was Fish supposed to stay out of their grasp but also get close enough to steal their weapon?

Daniel handed him his cutlass. "Go for my stomach."

"Are you ready?" Fish asked.

"Yes. Now would you stop delaying and strike?"

Fish stepped forward and shot out his hand. Daniel clasped Fish's sword hand, then pulled the weapon toward him and moved to the side, jamming the blade into the wooden mast behind him. A terrible shock coursed through Fish's arm.

The cutlass was in deep; with all his strength Fish could not remove it. "How did you do that?"

"Anticipation. Study your opponent, predict what he's going to do next, and counterstrike. Here, watch, I'll do it slowly, then you try to disarm me."

Fish tried imitating Daniel, going a little faster with each repetition. The process was frustrating. Fish kept bumping into barrels and other obstacles, losing his balance.

"Part of your problem is comfort. You need to find your home on the ship. Your battlefield. Someplace that you know well and can use against your opponent."

"What is it for you?"

Daniel hesitated.

"I won't use it against you," Fish said. "We're friends. Right?"

"Pirates don't really have friends."

"What about the groups — Scab and his crew or the Scalawags for Sausage?"

"They are not friends. They are allies."

"What's the difference?"

"Allies share the same interests, but ultimately they live for themselves. If Scab had to choose between doubloons and Thimble's life, he'd choose the doubloons. Same with the One-eyed Willies and the Scalawags for Sausage. Even Cobb would probably ditch Melinda and Moravius for the right amount."

"That's not true!" Fish insisted.

"What do you know?" Daniel said. "You've been on the ship for a few weeks and you already know the captain better than I?"

"Well . . . I . . ."

There was no easy response. Daniel was obviously jealous. He did not like the idea that Fish might be more familiar with the captain. Yet Fish had spent those hours with him in the cabin and, according to Scab, few of the men had ever been in there for more than a minute or two. Fish also saw that there was a very real and deep bond between the giant, Cobb, and Melinda. The suggestion that the captain, too, was a coin-crazed rascal who valued treasure above love or friendship — it simply was not true. And Daniel needed to know that. "The night I was in the cabin, they didn't seem like mere allies."

"You say that like it's a bad word."

"The way you describe it, I think it is. To value yourself and money above all else? That's not what I saw. Not what I heard. They were more like a family." He thought about this for a moment. Certainly it stretched his definition of the term, but they were a family. "A small, strange family," he added, "but a family nonetheless."

Daniel held out his cutlass, a wordless warning that their lessons were to resume. He jabbed in at half speed, and Fish managed to yank Daniel's sword forward, but it missed the mast and jabbed a piece of sail instead.

"Try again. And remember: Know where you are."

They danced through the steps a second and third time with no success. Fish squeezed his eyes closed.

Daniel stopped. "You are thinking too hard. That slows you down, if you think and plan before you act. You don't think when you walk, do you?"

"No."

"When you swim?"

"No."

"Right," Daniel said. "And in a fight, or a not-fight, you don't think. You react."

As he pronounced the last word, Daniel jumped forward, thrusting his cutlass at full speed. Fish felt himself move to the side, watched his hands lash out, grab the hilt, and pull the sword backward, jamming it into the mast behind him. He almost couldn't believe what he'd done. He wasn't sure how it happened, or even what had happened, but the cutlass was stuck in the wood. Daniel had been disarmed.

Daniel laughed. "See? React. Don't think."

Part of Fish wished they could keep the cutlass there. The sight of it filled him with pride.

The two boys sat down and gazed up at the stars. Daniel had been good to him; he might not have been able to survive this far without him. If they weren't friends, he hoped at least that they were allies. "Hey, Daniel?" Fish asked.

"Yes?"

"You and me. Are we allies?"

"No, Fish, we're friends. And I'll prove it to you."

"Daniel, I trust you."

"And I'm going to place my trust in you, too, as a friend."

Daniel scurried under the steps leading up to the quarter-deck. "Here," he said, pointing to a small square panel in the wooden deck, in the darkness below the steps. "Open that."

Fish, on his knees in the small space, removed the panel.

"Go ahead, reach in," Daniel said.

His fingers closed around a cloth purse harboring something large and metallic. He picked it up, then moved into a beam of blue moonlight sneaking through the spaces between the steps. The purse was heavily embroidered and studded with small stones. He pulled out a silver key inlaid with gems matching those on the purse. "A key?"

"Not so loud!" Daniel whispered, checking to see whether anyone had heard. "Of course it's a key!"

"To what?"

"To my sea chest. Most pirates carry their keys around their necks. If you choose to hide it, you only reveal the location to your closest allies . . . or friends."

Fish slipped the key back in, then stared at the purse, admiring the embroidery, the tiny gems sparkling in the moonlight. The purse was a treasure in and of itself. "Why the fancy packaging?" he asked.

"An important item deserves elegant packaging, don't you think? The purse and its contents should be linked. Now," he said, changing his tone, "I can trust you, right?"

Fish should have shaken Daniel's hand, hugged him, or revealed some secret of his own to demonstrate that yes, he *could* be trusted, and that their bond was mutual. But his mind was stuck, fixed on Daniel's words: "The purse and its contents should be linked." Why did that statement strike him so?

"Fish? Fish? I can trust you, right? You're not going to grab my chest and try to pilfer any of my coins now, are you?"

That was it! The coins! The purse . . . Reginald Swift! Reginald Swift had been distraught when he learned that Fish hadn't brought the purse with him. Yet when Fish was in the cabin that night, he'd been so focused on examining the coins themselves that he'd forgotten about Reginald Swift's reaction. Perhaps the coins were only one part of the clue. Perhaps there was some sort of secret in the purse, too.

"Fish? I can trust you, right?"

Daniel had drawn closer, snapping Fish out of his reverie. "Yes! Yes, of course you can trust me. I'll never tell a soul. I swear. But now I have to go see the captain."

"The captain? Why?"

But Fish was gone, racing to the cabin, before Daniel had even finished his question.

HIDDEN KEY

He'd explain it all to Daniel later. He owed him at least that much after all his friend had taught him about boats, pirating, and the complex art of not-fighting. First, though, he had to study the purse to see if it really held some clue. Why else would Reginald Swift find it so important?

Fish burst into the captain's cabin. Cobb, Melinda, and Moravius were sitting together around the table, the coins stacked before them. "The purse!" he blurted. "Where is it?"

"What purse?" Cobb asked.

"The one that held the coins. Do you have it?"

Cobb looked at Melinda, who turned to Moravius, who relayed the exchange back to Cobb.

"We need to find it! I think it will help us make sense of the coins."

Cobb jumped to his feet, knocking into the table on his way up. "Scour the cabin!"

"The scouring would be easier if the two of you kept the place clean," Moravius said.

"Not now, you brute! Lift your inhuman frame out of that chair and help us."

The cabin was a wreck, so a few minutes passed before the giant discovered the purse under several stacks of leather-bound journals and books written in languages Fish did not recognize.

"Is this it?" he asked, tossing it to the boy.

The purse, emptied of its contents and pressed flat, was not much larger than one of his hands. Rectangular in shape, dark brown and aged, it had been made from a single piece of leather doubled over and sewn up along the seams. There was a metal clasp attached near the top to close it tight — simple twine would not have been enough to keep the coins from spilling out for so many years. Yes, it was definitely the same purse Uncle Gerry had given him. But how it would help him make sense of those coins, he could not imagine. "Why would Swift want this?" he asked aloud.

"Lady Swift?" Cobb pressed.

"No, her son, Reginald. Outside that cabin, aboard the *Mary*. When I showed him the coins, he was thrilled, but when he found out that I hadn't brought the purse, too, he despaired."

"Then the purse must hold some sort of clue," Cobb said.

Fish examined every fiber, every wrinkle. He studied the clasp, the seams running up along each side of the purse. Nothing. But what had he expected? Instructions? That would have been too simple. He'd begun to understand that few steps of a treasure hunt were easy.

"May I?" Cobb asked. He opened a drawer in his desk, fingered through a collection of eyeglasses, selected a pair of lenses that were nearly as thick as one of Sammy's fattened fingers, placed them on the bridge of his nose, and peered closely at the purse. "Nothing," he said after a moment. "No miniature messages or symbols."

Melinda studied the purse next, then Moravius, but not one of them noticed a single distinguishing feature. "What about the type of leather?" Moravius suggested. "Leather from a cow might have one meaning, from a pig another."

"But what sort of meaning?" Melinda asked.

They continued talking, passing the purse among them and offering new theories. Soon they began watching Fish, as if they were depending on him for a solution. Under their expectant stares, he picked up the purse, fumbled with it, felt along the seams. And then he turned it inside out.

"There!" Cobb yelled.

"How simple!" Moravius added.

Melinda excitedly wrapped Fish in her thick arms.

There were several circular imprints burned into the leather, each with a small icon in the center. The flower, the bird, the knife — they were all there. The icons on the twenty-nine coins matched the purse. This was why Reginald Swift wanted it!

Hands shaking with anticipation, Fish laid the purse on the table, flattened it out. There were six circles lined up in a row on one side; he flipped it over and counted six on the other, too. A single line ran below them, or above, depending on which way he held the purse. If he could tear open the seams along either side, he would have a single strip of leather with those imprints in a single row. But he lacked the strength to pull it apart. This purse had remained intact through years of wear and travel; it wasn't going to succumb to his small hands. Besides, there was an easier way. "Melinda," he said, "do you have your knife?"

He handed her the purse and she carefully cut along each stitched side.

Now Fish had before him a large band of leather, about twice as long as one of his hands. The two sets of six circles were arranged in a straight line. A simple dash separated them in the middle, where the bottom of the purse had been folded. Another, longer line stretched below the circles. He rotated it so that this line was on top, then switched back.

"It must be a series," Melinda decided. "In which case that line should be on the bottom. That way, we know which circle is meant to be first."

The first circle featured an icon of a serpent, the second a bird. In the middle of the third, there was an image of a tree, in the fourth a knife, in the fifth a lion, then a flower, a horse, a boat, and, in the ninth position, a crown. Finally, in the last three circles, one of the elements was repeated: Each of them contained a simple picture of a flower, just like the sixth.

Could it be that easy? That last night in the cabin, Fish had stacked the coins according to the same icons. But none of them could determine how to arrange those piles. Two of the coins bore the icon of the serpent, so Fish moved this short stack into that first circle. In the next circle there was a bird, so he picked up the corresponding stack of coins and moved the pair into position.

Next he looked for the coins bearing the image of the tree and placed another stack of two into the third circle. A stack of three coins filled the fourth circle, all of them with the symbol of a knife. Three coins matched the lion in the fifth position, four fit with the flower in the sixth spot. He placed seven coins into the seventh circle, three into the eighth, and another stack of three into the ninth.

At the tenth position, Fish stopped, sat back, and stared. No coins remained. Yet each of the last three circles shared the same icon as the sixth: the flower. Had he erred somehow? Yes! He'd placed that stack of four coins into a single circle when he should have distributed them evenly amongst those four circles — one of the flower coins in each of the four corresponding circles.

He was finished. But with what? The stacks of coins, neatly arranged in a row, ranging in height from one to seven, were hardly a map. They didn't exactly provide directions.

"What about the golden coins?" Moravius asked. "Might they fit in here somehow?"

"No," Cobb answered. "They are decoys. That much is clear now. Focus on these stacks, Moravius."

The giant did as he was told, and within seconds he clapped with excitement. "Brilliant!"

"*What* is brilliant?" Cobb asked.

"Don't you see? Six here, six there?"

The captain did not see. Neither did Melinda nor Fish.

Moravius knelt next to Fish at the edge of the desk and began counting the coins in each stack. "Two, two, two, three, three, one. Then seven, three, three, one, one, one."

Cobb's face was blank. "And?"

"Think!" Moravius said.

"I am thinking!" Cobb fired back.

"Consider them in pairs. Two-two, then two-three, and then three-one. Then seven-three, three-one, one-one."

"If it's a verse from Homer or Ovid you may as well tell us," Melinda sighed.

"No!" Moravius said. "Latitude and longitude!"

Cobb's eyes opened wide. "Of course! Twenty-two hours, twenty-three minutes, thirty-one seconds by seventy-three hours, thirty-one minutes, eleven seconds."

Fish had heard the terms before — he remembered Daniel mentioning them while explaining how the captain knew where they were in the vast ocean. "So these numbers, they're like an address?"

"Yes, the address!" Cobb shouted. "Given a line of latitude and a corresponding line of longitude, we can find any point on the globe! You may very well have discovered the location that has eluded countless treasure hunters!"

"One problem," Moravius said. He was hunched over a map of the world. "Seventy-three longitude is on the other side of the Earth."

They heard a noise just outside the cabin — as if someone or something had fallen. Cobb nodded to Moravius, and the giant stepped quietly and quickly to the door, then thrust it open. He ducked and moved out onto the deck, inspecting the area. A small bucket lay overturned nearby — it must have fallen from the steps leading up to the quarterdeck.

Moravius held it up for Cobb to see, shrugged, and came back inside.

Cobb moved over to the line of coins and shifted his wig. Fish watched his brow tighten. The captain pushed his fist against his forehead, just above his long nose. And then he smiled.

"What is it?" Moravius asked.

Cobb was glowing. "Do you mean you don't know? But it is *so* apparent. A simple —"

"Enough! Tell me."

"Cease gloating, Walter," Melinda added.

Cobb pointed to the dash imprinted in the leather. "Not seventy-three. Negative seventy-three!"

If only they'd explain themselves. "What does that mean?" Fish interrupted.

"It means we're close! We'll sail north from Turtle Island, then a week's sail from there, at most."

"Close to what?"

"The Chain of Chuacar!"

COBB'S QUEST

Fish wanted answers. He felt he was entitled to at least one or two after all he'd done, so he addressed Cobb: "The men have been talking about the chain, but I'm not sure who to believe. I've heard so many stories . . . what's the truth?"

Melinda and her husband exchanged a glance. Cobb walked over to his desk, opened a drawer, pulled out some tobacco, and stuffed it into his pipe. Then he removed an object wrapped in cloth and placed it in his pocket. "Come up to the quarterdeck with me, Fish, and I will tell you all about it."

The wind was steady but quiet that night, and the *Scurvy Mistress* moved slowly through the waves. A bright half-moon shone in a cloudless sky.

For the first few minutes, the captain simply watched the water, quietly smoking his pipe. There were a million questions Fish wanted to ask, but his uncle Gerry had taught him not to interrupt a man while he's smoking, so he kept his mouth closed.

Finally, Cobb spoke. "Melinda, Moravius, and I have been searching for the Chain of Chuacar for more than ten years. Almost as long as you've been alive. We found our first clue by accident. We were raiding the *Dulcinea*, a Spanish galleon outside of . . . what?"

"Sorry," Fish said, "but what's a galleon?"

"Have you not read your *Guidelines* yet?"

"I've been too busy —"

"One is never too busy to read, young man. Galleons are massive, stout ships that can be outfitted for battle or commerce. Very challenging to win one on account of all their guns. We tracked this one through a storm and sailed up quiet, in the middle of the night, in a fog as thick as milk. Once our men boarded the ship, the crew gave up quietly, without much of a fight. We searched the hold for an hour, found only a few chests of gold, and carried them onto the *Scurvy Mistress*. It was a nice prize, enough gold to keep us supplied with food and gunpowder for a year or more, and I was ready to sail off once we had it on board. But then I noticed the captain of the other ship was smiling."

"Why was he smiling if he'd been raided?"

"Exactly my thought. This man had no reason to smile. Unless, of course, we'd missed something. So I took the captain by the arm and, with Moravius at my side, led him into his cabin. I asked him politely if he had anything else of value on board, and he said no. So I asked Moravius to shake the answer out of him. Well, Moravius hadn't laid a finger on the man before he revealed everything. He had a map, he said, a clue to the location of the Chain of Chuacar, and he was supposed to bring it back to the king of Spain himself. From his desk he pulled a small, faded piece of parchment."

"A map?"

"Yes, and it led us to a limestone cave near Port Regal, a popular pirate city. It also included a small sketch of a be-jeweled knife. We assumed at the time that this was purely decorative, but after searching the cave, we uncovered a trea-sure chest — a mediocre haul, really, but enough to satiate the men. Yet there was a heavily ornamented knife packed inside that matched the sketch exactly."

"But you didn't find the chain."

"No, and I had made the mistake of telling the men we were searching for it. If we hadn't discovered that chest, there might have been a mutiny."

"If you only found the knife and some treasure, why did you keep looking?"

Cobb laughed. "That's a bigger question, with a much longer answer than I think you'd care to hear, Fish. But our quest did continue. Nearly two years later, Melinda was pol-ishing the knife when the bottom of the handle sprang open. Another map fell out. Instead of a knife, this one bore a pic-ture of a medallion."

"You found that, too, I assume."

"Of course! Naturally, we were smarter that time and declined to tell the men of our true aims. But we found the medallion and, disguised on its face, another map. Over the last ten years we've traveled all over the world, moving from one clue to the next, hoping that we have been getting closer to the chain. And all that time we've struggled to keep our men satisfied."

"This is what Scab was yelling about when I first came on the boat, right? He knew that the coins were part of your quest for the chain?"

"Correct. Scab is no fool, and men like him can only be duped for so long. Plenty of food and beer sates their appetites for a while, but eventually they crave gold, and we have to provide them with it. That is why we are forced to conduct the occasional raid. We need to fill their coffers. Yet even with those diversions, we continued our search. We found two more maps, a small spyglass that offered hints of its own and, finally, we learned of these coins."

"How *did* you find out about them?" Fish asked. He'd been wondering how his uncle Gerry was involved. "You said that my uncle works with pirates . . ."

"I did, yes. I'm sure he has other interests, too, but any merchant in any port town conducts business with pirates on occasion. Bakers sell us their bread, brewers their beer. This does not make them brigands, too. Nevertheless, Reidy Merchants are known agents in our world."

"The pirate world?"

"No, the world of treasure hunting in particular. We are not the only ship of our kind, as I'm sure you know, and we are not the only people in search of the chain, either. There are other pirates, like ourselves, and landed folk, too, who hire pirates and adventurers to search out these treasures for them."

"Such as Reginald Swift and his mother," Fish guessed. The tiny man could not have been a pirate himself.

"Correct. His mother, that frustratingly immortal harpy who insists on calling herself Lady Swift, is a very renowned, successful, and utterly ruthless treasure hunter. Do not let her grandmotherly appearance deceive you. That woman is a viper. How she caught on to our quest I do not know, but I do know *when* she became involved. A few months ago, that spyglass I mentioned led us to a small island off Greece. Yet when we arrived, we found that another crew had already come and gone with the coins. We managed to track the men and learned they were hired by Reidy Merchants."

Fish couldn't believe it. "So my uncle employs pirates?"

"In a way, yes, but he's merely an agent. Lady Swift paid him to organize a crew to retrieve the coins. They nearly succeeded, too, if not —"

"If Nate hadn't grabbed them from me," Fish said.

Cobb put a hand on his shoulder. "That was not your fault," he said. "If Nate hadn't succeeded, we would have taken them anyway, once the *Mary* left port. Besides, Lady Swift is no longer any concern of ours. She is weeks behind us in our search, if not months. She has neither the coins nor a sharp young man like yourself to decipher their meaning."

As Cobb smoked, Fish tried to make sense of all he'd heard. The story of the adventure was marvelous, the prospect of continuing that quest just as exciting. But he still had questions. And he would ask them, even if the captain had resumed puffing on his pipe. "You said you've followed these clues all over the world?"

"Correct."

"But from what I heard, only one man knew the location of the chain."

"An English explorer and adventurer. Wentworth Collins."

"If that's true, why would Collins go to such lengths, hiding hints across the oceans? Why wouldn't he just tell someone eventually? He could have informed someone powerful, who might have helped him remove the chain from its hiding place. He could have died rich."

"Treasure hunters are a strange and inexplicable group of people, Fish! We spend years, decades, entire lives searching for glorious, legendary riches that may not exist. We will never know how Collins himself discovered the chain, but I suspect that he struggled mightily in his quest, and found the idea of someone else uncovering that treasure without an equally significant struggle too deplorable to bear. Consider those coins."

"The ones in the stacks, you mean?"

"Yes! Imagine: A single man commissioned the production of twenty-nine entirely different coins. This must have been a painstaking and complicated task — truly the work of a man obsessed! A man more interested in the search for treasure than treasure itself."

Cobb's theories about Collins only stirred more questions. "But what if it's all a trick? How do you know whether Collins left real hints to the location of the chain? And even if the quest he laid out is an honest one, how can you be certain these coins are not merely another clue?"

The captain sucked in on his pipe. "We can't be certain. But do you remember the profile on the golden coins?"

"Yes," Fish answered. "A queen, with a crown, and an enormous chain wrapped around her neck. But I thought we decided they were decoys?"

"They could have *some* signficance, even if they don't offer a direct clue to the location. We believe that profile is a representation of Chuacar's wife. It is a strong indication that we are close to finding the chain itself, not merely another map."

This worried Fish. The crew suspected they were in search of the chain; if they found out that Cobb wasn't absolutely certain they'd find it, mutiny would be a very real possibility indeed.

"The men won't be —"

"You may leave the concerns of the men to me," Cobb said firmly.

After another long draw on his pipe, Cobb took out the package he'd removed from his desk. "I have something for you," he said, handing it to Fish.

Wrapped in the cloth, he found a strange pair of eyeglasses — two large, round pieces of glass framed in wood, then cushioned with waxed leather. Cloth ties dangled off each side.

"Thank you, sir . . . but what are they?"

"They're swimming glasses! For Fish the pirate."

The captain placed the glass circles over Fish's eyes and tied the straps behind his head. The wooden rims and bridge held the glass away from his eyes, and the leather cushioned the wood so it didn't press into his skin.

"Wear them underwater. They must be tight or water will leak in. I have had them for a long, long time but never found much use for them myself. Melinda and I decided that if you are so drawn to the water, you might as well see what the world looks like down there."

Fish didn't know what to say. Back home, the only presents he received were particularly well-shaped potatoes or patches of cloth to cover new holes in his pants. No one had ever given him anything fun. He managed to say "thank you" a few times, then stood with the goggles still on his face, gazing out at the dark water. He wanted to dive in right then and there.

Cobb started chuckling. "You can take them off now, Fish. You will have plenty of opportunities to test them where we are going."

Slightly embarrassed, Fish coughed and stared out again at the open water. Bright stars filled the entire sky, straight down to the horizon.

"I believe there is a reason you came to our ship," Cobb said. "I believe you have great potential."

"Potential?"

"You could make a great treasure hunter one day, perhaps a great captain, too."

In Fish's head a vision appeared: He was standing on the bridge of the *Scurvy Mistress*, much older, with a pipe in his hand and a huge scar across his forehead. It was an odd scene, and not altogether believable. "A pirate captain?"

"That is for you to decide. You must never let anyone else

tell you who you are. A man must determine his place in the world on his own."

"I'm not sure I could ever control a group like this," Fish said.

"No one can," Cobb answered. "A good captain doesn't control his men. He leads them."

"Is there a difference?"

"Of course! I do not order the men to follow me. I allow them to choose. If I lead effectively, they will see no choice but to follow."

"But leading a man like Scab is impossible. He counters your every suggestion."

Cobb removed his knife, ran the blade carefully down his jaw like a shaving razor. The metal gleamed in the moon-light. "Since the day seven years ago when we captured his ship, I have been watching Scab's every move, knowing full well that he could start a mutiny at any time."

"If the risk is so great, why keep him on? Why make him your second in command?"

"Because he's one of the most skilled swordsmen I've ever seen. He is absolutely fearless and a brilliant sailor; he could handle this ship himself if need be. Sailing across the world, dodging naval ships, is no easy task. It requires a crew, and men like Scab, too. Furthermore, I would rather have him on board the *Scurvy Mistress* as part of my crew, where I can watch him, than sailing his own sloop. If he were to leave, he'd probably raid us within a matter of weeks.

"You see, Fish, Scab is a different breed than Moravius, Melinda, and myself. There are really two sides to the pirate business. One involves plundering ships."

"The raids," Fish said.

"Right. The true raider, like Scab, is only interested in capturing prizes. That is how most pirates measure success. Admiral Blood, for example; most pirates would rank him as one of the top three or four buccaneers of all time because they say he took two hundred ships in only two years."

Fish's eyes widened. That would mean a new raid every few days.

"Yes, Blood's feat was very impressive. But let me ask you this: Who was he stealing those ships from?"

Fish remembered the answer from the few pages he had read of *Guidelines for the Enterprising Pirate*: Most pirates attacked vessels belonging to one of three nations. "The Spanish, the English, or the Dutch."

"Exactly. The three most powerful nations in the world. Every few days, he was stealing a ship from at least one of them. Do you know what that fact means to me?"

"No . . ."

"It means he was making his enemies angrier and angrier every week. With every new prize, he gave those nations more reason to hunt him down. That's not my idea of a happy life, to be worried all the time that three of the most powerful countries on earth want nothing more than your head brought to them on a stake. That sort of pirate can never stop and think. He needs to keep moving. He needs to keep capturing prizes."

"Scab."

"Exactly. If Scab had his way, we'd follow Blood's example, capturing every ship we saw. But I'm of a different breed. I'm a seeker, Fish. We take a prize now and then, to keep the men satisfied, but for the most part, we'd prefer to spend our efforts hunting down the treasure that the Scabs of the world are too wild and restless to search for themselves."

Cobb gazed out at the water. A wide beam of blue-white moonlight played on the surface, like a path leading straight to the edge of the earth. The captain yawned and announced that it was time to sleep.

"Captain?" Fish said.

"Yes?"

"I think I'm a seeker, too."

Cobb smiled. "Yes, Fish. I think you are."

FESTERING SCAB

Two weeks had passed since Fish's conversation with Cobb. Two weeks packed with deck swabbing, not-fighting, learning about knots, judging eye patches, discussing the optimal degree of saltiness in salami, finally reading more than a few pages of *Guidelines for the Enterprising Pirate*, and, whenever possible, sleeping. In all, he had been on the *Scurvy Mistress* just two months, but he felt like he'd been there for the whole of his life. He couldn't remember what it felt like to stand on solid, unwavering ground.

Fish was scrubbing the floor beside the galley one morning when the men began cheering and yelling. Nora raced out, green eyes bright with energy. She brushed her hands on her dress, which was, given its tattered condition and abundant stains, really just one large apron. "Quick!" she said. "I think they've spotted land!"

They rushed up to the deck and hurried to the edge of the boat with the rest of the crew. The land was little more than a lump on the horizon. He couldn't discern many details, but the water! The water was absolutely beautiful. In only a day the color had changed from dark green to crystal-clear blue. The sun was stronger, too. Altogether it felt like another world.

He ran up to the bow and leaned over. Three porpoises — Nora and Daniel had to tell him what they were, since he'd never seen anything like them — were diving in and out of the water, playing in front of the boat as it cut through the small waves. The long journey, the terrible food, the endless days spent in the stinking, filthy quarters below — it had all been worthwhile.

Noah and the men began singing:

Land ho
Land ho
Where the trees and flowers grow
And the ocean's waves don't flow
Land ho
Land ho

The mood changed from the first sighting of solid ground; the men worked and sang with added vigor and even fought with a kind of playfulness. At first, Fish assumed it was the prospect of planting their feet on dry earth that excited the men, or the idea of sleeping on a mat that didn't roll and swing like a hammock, but Daniel explained that it wasn't land in general that drew out such joy, but a particular location. They were up top at the time, with Nora and Nate and much of the crew. A few days had passed since the first sighting of land and they were now between islands, the horizon blank before them.

"It's called Turtle Island and it's a pirate paradise," Daniel said. "The harbor is guarded by six big guns mounted high on the cliffs to keep out unwanted visitors. There are four inns, five pubs, and the best food you'll ever eat. Palm trees handmade by God to shade you from the sun during a midday sleep. And the goods and trinkets! The sharpest knives, the most reliable pistols, anything you want you'll find on Turtle Island."

"Thimble always drinks the place dry of wine, then buys all the linens and silks they have so he can make his fancy shirts and scarves," Nate said.

"Sammy the Stomach buys more sausage than you could eat in a year," Nora said.

"You can get an adjustment at Dr. Doubloons," Nate added.

"What's an adjustment?" Fish asked.

"Most pirates have crooked backs from sleeping in hammocks all the time," Daniel explained. "There's a kind of doctor on Turtle Island who can crack your back and readjust your spine. Makes you feel like new."

This sounded intriguing, but the prospect of a good meal, soft bread, perhaps a potato or two, was far more enticing. "You mentioned food," Fish said. "Do you have a favorite place to eat?"

"The Salty Scabbard," Nate offered, "has perfectly cooked crabs."

Nora agreed, then added, "The monkey stew at the Rusty Anchor is wonderfully spicy."

"And you can't leave without dipping a spoon in the turtle soup at Dancing Dan's," Nate urged. "They slow cook it because that's how the turtles swim."

"A perfect mix of salty and sweet, too," Nora added.

"What about you, Daniel? Any favorites?" Fish asked.

At first Daniel didn't answer. "Never been there," he said after a moment. "I haven't been off the boat in five years. The last time I put my feet on land, there was a tempest in my stomach. The rolling of a ship at sea is my stability; without it I become violently ill. Some people get seasick, I suffer from land-sickness. But you'll bring me back a few items, a morsel or two, won't you? I'll give you a list."

"Of course I will," Fish answered.

The *Scurvy Mistress* sailed for three more long days before Daniel, perched atop the mast early one morning and staring toward a horizon blurred by fog, shouted, "Turtle Island ahead!"

Holding on to his swab, Fish rushed to the side of the boat with the other men, who were ready to dance with glee. Noah broke into song:

> *Where the trees are bright and green*
> *And the ladies fine and clean,*
> *I'll rest there for a good long while,*
> *Spend my gold on Turtle Isle.*

Fish heard the men say they were at least an hour away. It would have been wonderful to remain on deck, but he knew he'd be expected to resume his work down below. Before he'd taken two steps in that direction, though, a hand clamped down on his shoulder.

Without thinking he reacted, dropping nearly to his knees, turning his shoulders, and stepping aside. The lessons with Daniel were working! He had slipped away. He'd moved *with* the person who tried to grab him, instead of trying to pry the hand off. And he had done it without thinking.

This was a positive development, but the owner of the hand, Scab, was hardly ready to issue congratulatory remarks. He despised everything Fish did. But what had Fish done now?

Thimble, standing behind Scab, said, "Impressive!"

"An important development, considering our destination," Scab added.

"Why's that?" Fish asked.

"Because Turtle Island is not all delicious food and fun," Scab said. "An island full of pirates means an island full of fighting. Your crewmates" — he pointed to Thimble — "will defend you, of course, should you become involved in a scuffle. But we will not always be there. You will need to learn how to defend yourself, too."

Though his words suggested he was interested in helping Fish, the tone of the conversation was all wrong. Fish held up his swab and started to walk away. "Thank you for the warning, but I should resume my duties."

"Now is not the time for swabbing decks!" Scab said, the metallic hoops stuck through his face shining in the sunlight. "First we must see if you are prepared for what might face you on Turtle Island."

"May I?" Thimble asked, placing his hand on the hilt of his cutlass.

"No," Scab answered. "Allow me."

The first mate raised his fists.

Scab wanted him to fight. But Fish refused. "No," he said, backing away, "this will hardly be necessary."

Scab's thick fist, large enough to fit on a man twice his size and with countless tarnished rings jammed between the knuckles, flashed forward. Again, without thinking, Fish ducked his head. The punch merely grazed his ear. Scab, snarling, his face knotted behind his ragged beard, stepped back and raised his fists once more. Those rings! Fish feared them more than the pirate's cutlass. They'd leave dents in his forehead.

Scab swung from another angle. Fish dodged it and stepped away. He had to keep talking, try to reason with him. "Really, I don't think it's necessary to test me. You are obviously a far more skilled fighter and —"

"You do not decide what is and is not good for you!" Scab shouted. "Any ship is only as strong as its weakest rib, and you, boy, are the weakest rib!"

Quickly, Fish studied his surroundings. Find where you're comfortable. That's what Daniel had said. Unfortunately, he still had not figured that out. The stairs to the quarterdeck were back over his right shoulder, the mast a few paces ahead, three barrels to his left. Where was he comfortable? Nowhere.

But this open space was no good. He'd feel better with something behind him. The barrels, perhaps. Fish moved toward them. "I promise to avoid all conflicts on shore," he suggested. Scab punched again and missed. "Really," Fish said, "I am rather good at avoiding conflict."

Several men had begun following them now, and Fish's response produced a few eruptions of laughter. He glanced around; more members of the crew were walking over to watch. Nate and Daniel were among them, but he knew they could not intervene. This would be Fish's fight to win or lose. No, his fight to avoid.

Slow and deliberate, Scab pulled his cutlass from his belt. "Go on," he said, pointing the tip at Fish's waist.

Was he asking him to remove his own sword? "I don't have one," Fish said, "and I don't need one."

They continued to circle each other. Scab would not be talked down. There were too many people watching now, and he wouldn't stand to be embarrassed.

But perhaps Fish could convince Scab to lay down the cutlass. "I don't see why you need one. I am merely a boy."

"Cut the little rat!" someone yelled. It sounded like Jumping Jack.

The cheer was discouraging, until several more men responded in Fish's favor.

"Pick that Scab, Fish!"

"Drain that pile of pus!"

These shouts gave Fish confidence, and they also seemed to weaken Scab's resolve. The pirate began to sheathe his weapon. Fish felt his tense legs relax. He had stopped the fight without a punch.

Fish looked to Daniel, his friend and teacher, for approval. But in place of pride, urgency burned in his friend's bright eyes. Scab stopped and sneered, revealing his cracked brown teeth. The cutlass flew back out and he leaped at Fish, holding him up against a barrel with the blade pressed to his throat. Fish felt the rough black hairs of the pirate's beard against his skin.

Scab was not going to kill him, but it felt as if he'd already completed the fatal stab. After all those lessons with Daniel, all those nights of not-fighting, Fish had not reacted in time. The men were booing. Daniel, Nate, Nora, and even Cobb would be disappointed.

Scab was right. He was the weakest rib.

The pirate sheathed his blade and grabbed Fish's hair as if he were pulling a clump of weeds out of a field. Fish screamed, closed his eyes, and tried to yank Scab's hand away, but there was no unleashing that grip. Nothing that Daniel had taught him could save him now.

Fish stumbled, struggling to keep pace as the pirate pulled him across the deck, every misstep causing Scab to pull harder on his hair. Then, finally, he released him.

They were at the railing. The men were all to his right. To his left stretched the clear blue sea. Scab grabbed him by the shirt, pulled him close, so they were face-to-face. Fish didn't even try to struggle. Scab's rancid breath burned in his nose. Fish tried to look away, to avoid the man's black eyes, bright red scars, and half-wrecked teeth.

"A fish, are you? Well, then, you should get off this boat and go back to where you belong. In the sea."

With that, Scab hoisted Fish over the side and dropped him into the water below. He splashed through the surface, descending in a torrent of bubbles, then stopped, hovering in the depths.

Short of breath, Fish swam hard to the surface. The boat was moving at a steady pace; he was already in its wake and he knew they wouldn't wait or come around. He didn't deserve their help or their sympathy.

Yet someone was gesticulating from the deck high above him. Moravius was there, pointing at something dangling down into the water. A line! He had thrown him a line. Fish swam toward it, up and over the small waves of the *Scurvy Mistress*'s wake. After a few more strokes, he grabbed the rope and, holding tight, he relaxed, allowing himself to collect his breath.

Up on the quarterdeck, Moravius was pulling on the line, bringing him closer. Fish took a few more breaths and shouted for the giant to stop. At that point, the *Scurvy Mistress* was the last place Fish wanted to be. He was safe in the water and, for a little while, that is where he would stay. Perhaps Scab was right. Perhaps the water was where he belonged.

TURTLE ISLAND

The sea rushed past him, slowly draining the sickening intensity of the fight from his body. The water was neither hot nor cold; it felt perfectly matched to his skin, as if he were part of it. And clear! The water was far deeper than the deepest part of Outhouse Lake and yet, even from above, at the wavy surface, he could see straight to the ocean floor.

Thinking of that undersea world, Fish remembered Cobb's gift. The swimming glasses! He reached down to his waist, untied them, and with the line wrapped around one arm, fastened the glasses around his eyes. A deep breath, then another, and he dropped down below the surface. The line dragged him through a multicolored underwater world full of purple, fernlike, waving plants, giant yellow rocks covered with small grooves and channels, fish of all shapes and colors and sizes. Thick, gray, menacing creatures kicked past schools of brightly striped minnows that darted and dodged in unison, as if they were all obeying the inaudible orders of some underwater captain. Only when it felt like Moravius was standing on his chest did Fish remember that he was not, in fact, one of these silvery minnows, but a boy who needed air to live. He kicked back up to the surface, sucked in a few restorative mouthfuls of air, and dove down once more.

Fish had been dragging behind the boat for at least an hour when the *Scurvy Mistress* cruised slowly into Turtle Island's heavily guarded harbor. The crew rowed for shore in the single launch, six men per trip. Thimble and Sammy the Stomach fought their way into the first boat, driven by extreme thirst and unmatched hunger, respectively. Later, Nate and Nora called down to Fish to see if he wanted to join them, but he declined. This was his first chance to swim in months, and he had never seen so much life and color. He pulled off his shirt, tied the arms tight around his waist, swam and dove around the harbor for a while longer before crawling up onto the flourlike white sand.

His shoulders and back felt burned by the sun. Fish stumbled from the water's edge to a grove of odd trees with tall, skinny, branchless trunks stretching up to a thin canopy of leaves. The trees reminded Fish of a lady's parasol — they had to be the palms Daniel had mentioned, the ones designed by God for napping. He stretched his shirt out to dry in the sun, lay down on the shady sand with his eyes aimed up at the slowly rocking tops, and fell into a heavy and dreamless sleep.

Evening had arrived when Fish awoke. His stomach growled, demanding food. What had Nora said was her favorite place? The Salty Scabbard? No, that was Nate's. The Rusty Anchor? Yes, that's where he'd go first. Fish eased to his feet and understood instantly why Daniel preferred to stay aboard. His head spun, his stomach switched from ravenous to queasy. The solid ground was now as alien to him as the rocking deck of the boat had been when they first set sail. He'd have to move slowly and give himself time to adjust.

A dirt path led up and out of the harbor. He shook the sand off his dry, salt-encrusted shirt and started walking. At the top of the hill, the path opened into a large town square crowded with people. The smells were incredible: sizzling charred meats, burning spices, baking breads, the sweetness of many-flavored soups and stews.

Strangers crowded the square. He'd never seen them before, yet they were familiar. They were, after all, pirates: loud, dirty, ragged, and rude. Among them a pair of One-eyed Willies sat with their arms around each other, gripping great silver mugs overflowing with grog and singing to the rising moon.

A series of buildings surrounded the square, each one belching songs and shouts and cheers through wide-open windows and doors. There was the Salty Scabbard to his right, the Rusty Anchor straight ahead, and Dancing Dan's next to that. The men inside Dancing Dan's were singing and drinking, carousing and eating, and fighting. There were more women in the crowd than he expected, but they did not have a civilizing effect on the pirates.

A horde burst from the doorway, rushing out like sheep loosed from a pen. Noah was in the throng, greasy hair hanging free, pencil and nails still stuck behind his ears. Bat,

Owl, and Simon were just behind him. Then he eyed Nate and Nora. Still ashamed by his performance on the *Scurvy Mistress*, Fish shied away, but they stopped him.

"You did fine," Nate said. "Remember, Scab is a skilled fighter. Next time you'll not-fight him to sleep."

"Where have you been?" Nora asked.

"Swimming."

"Well, now is the time to eat," Nate said.

"How about that place?" Fish asked, pointing to the Rusty Anchor.

"Great! That's where they have the monkey stew," Nora said.

"Oh . . ."

"And gorgeous beef, too, if you prefer something traditional. Roasted on a spit with a garden's worth of herbs."

That sounded far better than monkey. "Perfect."

The origin of the pub's name was evident immediately. In the middle of the room lay a massive, rusted anchor, lying there as if cut loose from some sky-going ship. They ordered a monkey stew, roasted pig, and a serving of beef. Fish set in right away when the plates arrived. The beef was blackened on the outside, encrusted with charred herbs, emanating smells he could not describe, and moist in the center. He devoured the first bite, then several more, before noticing that Nora and Nate were staring. "What?"

"It's as if you haven't eaten in weeks."

In fact, that was exactly how he felt, but of course he couldn't say this aloud. "No, it's not that —"

"Stop," Nora said. "I won't be offended. Monkey stew?"

He tested a spoonful and, despite his initial hesitancy, found it to be nearly as delightful as the beef, though it proved slightly stringy and took more effort to chew. The roasted pig, though, was his favorite. On special occasions, they enjoyed pork on the farm, but it had never tasted like this, so sweet and fall-apart delicious. Two mouthfuls into his first plate, he ordered a second.

They sat for what felt like hours, eating, talking, telling stories. Nora spoke of her longing to get out from behind that galley counter, perhaps even open a pub of her own in a more refined port. Nate hoped aloud that he'd be a great captain one day.

"You will," Nora said. "I know it."

He blushed at the comment, then quickly stood up from the table to conceal his embarrassment. "I'll settle our account."

"No, you don't —" Nora began.

"Please, allow me," Nate said.

Fish began to object, too, then stopped and laughed.

"What is it?" Nate asked.

"I ordered two plates of pork, two servings of beef, a bowl of monkey stew, and I don't know how many glasses of milk."

"And?"

"And I don't have a single coin to my name."

"Soon enough, your sea chest will be full," Nate said. "Soon enough."

The next three days were packed with hard work. From first light until nearly dusk, with only an hour's rest at noon,

Fish was in the water, scraping the hull free of barnacles and sea greenery. He'd forgotten that this was one of the tasks Cobb had mentioned when he was assessing whether Fish would be a suitable member of the crew. All the weeds and crustaceans that accumulated over a year of neglect had begun to slow the ship. Without them, the hull would cut more smoothly through the seas.

Fish understood the value of the work, but this did not lessen the pain. His hands and fingers cramped, the muscles pulling them into unnatural alignments. His lungs ached from holding his breath. And he was probably going to have permanent depressions around his eyes from wearing his swimming glasses all day.

Daniel and Nate worked on the boat, filling the seams with oakum and pitch to prevent leaks. Nora was busily restocking. With Foot and a few of his assistants, she'd purchase new supplies, including barrels of flour and drink, ferry them out to the *Scurvy Mistress*, then lock them in the storeroom next to her galley. The lock was there to prevent the pirates from drinking more than their share of wine, rum, or grog, but Nora showed Fish, Daniel, and Nate where she hid the key. She said she felt bad for them, working on the ship while most of the crew enjoyed the town. This way, they could sneak an extra bite to eat when needed.

The days were long, but the evenings were delightful. After finishing for the day, Fish would swim ashore and eat with Nate and Nora at the Rusty Anchor. The other pubs were too rough and rowdy, and the food, Nora said, was no better. Afterward they'd row the launch back out to the *Scurvy Mistress* and sit on the deck with Daniel, telling stories and talking piracy. Daniel proved to be a true historian of their culture. He knew all there was to know about the great raiders and treasure hunters, and quite a bit about the obscure ones, too. Before long, his friends knew Fish's entire history as well: the farm, Outhouse Lake, his brothers and sisters, his gruff father and stern, strong mother, and his mysterious uncle Gerry. It felt good to tell them. It made him feel less alone.

Nearly all of the pirates slept ashore, so on these nights, the four friends felt like lords of the ship, kings and queen of the sea. With the moon and stars bright in the night sky, the water flat and calm, the leaves of the tree-lined shore dancing in the light breeze, Fish thought he'd entered paradise.

On the morning of the fourth day, Fish dove in to find that the hull was perfectly clean. Any more attention from his scraping blade and he'd be scratching off cedar. Cobb happened to be on board at the time.

"And only three days!" he said when Fish gave his report. "Good work, my boy. Take today to enjoy the island."

A week earlier, his chosen form of leisure would have been firmly aquatic, but after spending the majority of his last three days in the harbor, he wanted to feel the earth beneath his feet. Nora had said the walk to the top of Turtle Island's highest point was rewarding, so he proposed the hike to his friends.

"A marvelous idea," Nora replied.

"I'll bring a bow," Nate added. "I've heard there's prized game in the hills."

"And you?" Fish asked Daniel.

His land-averse friend shook his head.

After rowing ashore, Nate bought a small bow and a quiver of arrows from Dolphin Dry Goods, the island's general store. Nora, whose normally pale skin had begun to tan from a few days out in the sun, bought herself a hat, and the three of them marched off into the woods.

From the start, Nate was quiet and vigilant, as if a great lion could emerge at any second. He was trying to impress Nora, but she needed no convincing. The way she watched him, admiring his careful eye, Fish could see that their attraction was mutual. She was perpetually adjusting her long blond hair.

Still, the bow and arrow display did strike him as strange. They were supposed to be seafarers, not hunters. Before long he couldn't resist pointing out the contradiction. "You are a pirate," he said. "A man of the sea. Why are you acting like a woodsman?"

Eyes forward, Nate replied, "One could argue that this is piracy in its purest form, the very origin of our culture."

"How so?"

"Have you not read your Black?"

"No," Fish answered, recalling that Cobb, too, had suggested he read Phineas Black's *Concise History of Caribbean Marauding.* Then, recalling Nate's aversion to books, he asked, "Have you?"

"No, but Daniel did, and he told me the word 'buccaneer' comes from the French term *boucan*."

"A sort of frame for smoking meat," Nora added. "I've heard the results are delightful."

"The earliest Caribbean rovers were men who hunted wild boar on islands like this one, smoked them over fire pits, then sold them to the citizens of nearby colonies."

"They were hunters?" Fish asked, surprised.

"They were hunters," Nate answered.

"And we remain so," Nora said, "only now we hunt for gold."

As they climbed, the trees became shorter and thicker, their leaves boasting a deeper shade of green. It had rained the night before and although the town had since dried, everything here was still wet.

The branches of the trees intertwined to form a canopy overhead, a green and leafy ceiling. Thin beams of sunlight pierced the gaps to illuminate their way.

They came to a clearing three-quarters of the way up the hill and stopped to view the vast turquoise sea flattened out behind them. Fish's gaze was drawn immediately to a well-traveled sloop with bright white sails nearing the entrance to the harbor. He had seen that boat before, after the raid of the *Mary*, when they'd returned to the *Scurvy Mistress* and raced away.

"She is familiar," Fish said.

"Yes," Nate answered, his voice solemn. "Yes, she is."

SWIMMING SPY

Once they spotted the mystery sloop, their day of leisure was over. They hurried back down to the square, resolved to inform another member of the crew. They saw Noah first, outside the Salty Scabbard, and told him what they'd seen.

"Should we tell the captain?" Fish asked.

A familiar growl interrupted their exchange. "Tell him what?"

A metal mug in one hand, the other resting on the hilt of his cutlass, Scab awaited an answer.

Fish didn't want to tell Scab. He didn't even want to look at the first mate. Not after their fight.

"The captain is not here. I am next in command. Tell me!"

Noah rubbed his flat face, as if to clear his head, and began, "The boys —"

"*And* the young lady," Nora interrupted.

"The boys and the young lady believe a ship has been following us."

"Impossible. Your childish eyes have deceived you. All sloops resemble one another from a distance. Furthermore, I highly doubt that any collection of timber could keep pace with the *Scurvy Mistress*. What shade are her sails?"

"White," Fish answered.

"The sloop we spied off Ireland had sails of linen, gray as storm clouds and as weathered as old Foot's wrinkled hands."

He was either wrong or lying. Daniel had described the sails clearly that day.

Scab took a long drink, then tossed his mug toward the door of the Salty Scabbard, nearly hitting Simon, who was stumbling out. "I'll bet my last share she's not the same, but I'll check nevertheless. Why don't you children" — he sneered — "scurry off and play."

As Scab staggered away, Noah shrugged and sauntered into the Salty Scabbard. But Scab's reaction hardly doused Fish's suspicions. In fact, it had the opposite effect. He not only believed that the sloop had followed them; he now believed that Scab was somehow involved.

But it was Nora who actually proved that something was amiss. "We did not say where the boat followed us *from*," she noted. "And we did not say that she was a *sloop*."

That evening, after they returned to the *Scurvy Mistress*, Fish decided to swim over to the mystery sloop for closer inspection. Daniel, Nate, and Nora protested, warning that he shouldn't go alone. But he had to; rowing the launch would be too noisy and none of them could swim.

His plan to approach unnoticed almost fell apart the moment he lowered himself into the water. The slightest movement of his hands or feet stirred up clouds of green, glowing dots in the dark water. He'd never seen anything like it.

"Don't worry," Daniel whispered from above. "They are harmless little bugs."

Bugs? The fact that he was swimming in a sea of luminescent bugs, regardless of how beautifully they glowed, was so repulsive that he nearly climbed straight back up onto the deck. But then he saw figures moving through the windows of the mystery sloop's cabin. Forget the bugs. He had to find out more about that boat.

As Fish swam, the moon snuck out from behind a wall of clouds. The surface of the harbor brightened, and the glow of the green bugs dulled. Not a soul was out on deck. Fish climbed up the anchor cable with surprising ease — a few weeks ago it would have been a struggle, but he was far stronger now — and crept back toward the quarterdeck. The cabin door was half open, so he hid himself out of view. He listened, but the wind muffled the voices. The only words he did hear: "Cobb should burn!"

The voice he couldn't place, but that was irrelevant. Now that he knew this was an enemy ship, he had to inform the captain.

A powerful gust of wind blew open the cabin windows and pushed open the door. Fish was startled, but he stifled the urge to flee, as the breeze carried with it a distinctive smell. A singular mix of rotting onions and unwashed feet.

Scab.

Someone stepped out to close the door. He was as wide and thick as Moravius, but not nearly as tall, and a mass of chains and jewelry hung from his neck.

Curiosity prevailed over prudence and, just before the boulderlike man closed the door, Fish poked out his head to risk one focused glimpse inside the cabin. He saw two men he did not recognize. And, with their backs to him . . . no, it couldn't possibly be them. Before he could be sure, the door closed.

He waited another few moments for the winds to die, hoping to make out some fragments of the conversation, but he heard nothing further. He left as quietly as he had come, then told the others what he'd heard — and smelled.

"We have to tell Cobb," Nora said.

"What?" Nate asked. "That he smelled Scab on another sloop?"

"But don't you think Cobb would want to know that someone wants him to burn?" Daniel asked.

As they argued, Daniel noticed a launch leaving the sloop. They resolved to wait until it had reached land, then follow the crew. Daniel rowed in with them and placed his hands on the dock as if he were ready to disembark.

"Come with us!" Fish urged.

But his friend had already lost faith. Simply holding the dock proved too much for him. "Not tonight," he said, his eyes filled with disappointment.

Up in the square, they saw one of the Tea Leaves wobbling toward them like a child learning to walk. "Ah, the little Irishman!" he shouted at Fish.

Fish took him by the shoulders and tried to avoid the man's rum-poisoned breath. "Have you seen Cobb?"

"I have! A moment ago."

But before telling them where he'd seen the captain, he collapsed to the ground, curled his knees up to his chest, and began to snore. In the wide-open window of the Rusty Anchor, behind the fallen Tea Leaf, Fish spied that boulderlike man he'd seen on the mystery sloop. He must have been wearing twenty or thirty necklaces. "Who is that?" Fish asked.

"That's Gustavo de Borges," Nate said. "He's the only five-time creeping champion in the history of the World Pirate Championships."

"Creeping? What in the world is that?"

"It's one of the main events," Nora explained, "and easily as competitive as knife throwing, singing, grog drinking, and line tying. In the creeping event, everything centers around the judge, a person of remarkable hearing —"

"The type who can hear a grasshopper hop," Nate jumped in. "The judge sits blindfolded in the middle of a large room. The floor is filled with twigs and branches and puddles of mud and gloop. The contestant has to creep across the floor toward the judge, making as little noise as possible. Most contestants get to within five or six steps at best before the judge hears them, but Gustavo is so good that he sits right down on the judge's lap before he knows he's there."

"Is he one of the men you saw?" asked Nora.

"He is," Fish answered.

"That is a bad sign indeed," Nate said.

Fish smirked. "Why? Because he can tiptoe?"

"Don't mock it," Nate answered. "He's also a widely feared raider. Creeping is a more valuable skill than you know."

"We've seen enough," Fish said. "Let's find Cobb."

They searched the Rusty Anchor and Dancing Dan's, pushing past men and women shouting in strange languages, but Cobb was nowhere to be found. They tried the Salty Scabbard next. Mugs flew over their heads as they entered. Beer splashed on Fish's neck. An enormously rotund woman nearly knocked him to the floor as she staggered for the door. Puddles of spilled drink lay everywhere, yet Fish stomped through them unbothered. His feet had already survived much worse on board the *Scurvy Mistress*.

Two scrawny pirates standing at a table just beside them were arguing over whether it was easier to pilfer from England or Spain. Some of the crew were there, too. Sammy the Stomach was leaning against a wall near the kitchen, shoving a whole crab, shell and all, into his mouth. Jumping Jack had attracted a small crowd of overweight pirates from another crew and was demonstrating the finer points of his exercises.

Then Fish spotted them. Cobb, Melinda, and Moravius sat at a corner table with an older couple he'd never seen before. Nate led the way to the captain's table.

"The future of piracy!" Cobb welcomed them. He was unusually joyful and lively. "Where's Daniel? Refused to disembark again, eh? A fascinating boy, Erasmus, you must hear more about him."

"Captain," Fish said, "we have some —"

"Manners, boy! I mean to introduce you to our very good friends, Mr. and Mrs. Erasmus Tallon. They established this haven, built it from the ground up."

"I was a pirate myself," the man said, "until the back went. You see, it's hard, as you get older, to sleep in hammocks. . . ."

Mr. Tallon continued talking about his ailments, but Fish couldn't listen. He couldn't just stand there as the storm clouds of mutiny gathered all around them, regardless of what good manners required. He appealed wordlessly to Moravius, but with no success. The giant's eyes were steeped in grog. But Melinda saw that Fish hadn't come over for casual banter. Cobb jumped slightly — she must have kicked him under the table.

"Excuse me, Erasmus," he said, interrupting his friend. "What is it, Fish?"

Fish started to speak, then stopped. This wasn't exactly something that should be said in a crowd. He didn't know whether this Erasmus person could be trusted.

Cobb saw his concern and pulled Fish aside, the mirth of the moment before fading from his face. "Tell me."

"A new sloop sailed in today. I believe it's the one that approached as we were raiding the *Mary*. So I snuck aboard —"

"You snuck aboard? Good man!"

"Yes, and I heard a few people inside, threatening to kill you."

"Our men?"

"I believe so. I'm fairly sure Scab was there —"

Cobb stopped him. "You are *fairly* sure?"

"Well, I . . ."

"What?"

He knew it would sound odd, but he had to be honest. "I smelled him," Fish said.

"You smelled him?"

"Yes, I know it sounds crazy, but Scab has a very distinctive odor, like old onions and —"

"Feet?"

"Yes!"

"I've noticed that myself, though I was never quite able to place the onion. But I must tell you, Fish, I need more than smells."

He wanted to tell Cobb who else he thought he'd seen, but he hadn't even told his friends. And he was not certain of it; he only had a glimpse into the dark cabin. He sounded ridiculous enough as it was, trying to reveal an impending mutiny based on a smell.

"I could send a man to walk the plank if mutiny were imminent, but you would have to be certain. Do you have any additional proof?"

Fish wished he could say yes, not to doom a man to death, but to stop a mutiny. Yet there was a chance he was wrong. Perhaps his thoughts had been colored by his bitterness toward Scab. He peered down at his feet, half submerged in a puddle of dark red liquid, then up at his captain. "No."

"I thank you for your concern," Cobb said. He put his arm around Fish's shoulders and led him back toward the table. "You must understand, though, that if I were to force every man to walk the plank when he threatens to burn, stab, or slice me, then I would have no one left to sail with. Such threats are an unfortunate part of life for a captain."

Cobb elbowed Moravius aside, clearing space for Nora, Nate, and Fish to join them at the table. "Erasmus," he said, "order these young people the best crab dinners your cook can muster!"

Then he whispered to Fish, "We will be on our guard."

THE SEARCH BEGINS

The very next morning, Cobb called the crew together on the beach. He stood in front of Moravius, who was holding the ship's flag high in the air, fastened to a cutlass, and waited until all were accounted for. Then he announced they'd be leaving by noon. Several of the men protested, but Fish was eager to depart. That sloop made him uneasy.

"Where to next, Captain?" Simon asked.

Jumping Jack pressed: "Will it be a raid?"

"A quest?" asked Noah.

"Another Turtle Island?" shouted Sammy the Stomach, prompting laughter from the men.

Cobb looked directly at Fish.

"We have, with the invaluable help of our new crew member, young Fish, discovered the location of a certain treasure of great value."

The men turned to Fish, and some looked at him approvingly. A few of the One-eyed Willies congratulated him with one-eyed winks. Fish tried to remain stern and serious, like the captain himself, but he could not resist smiling.

"As some of you have surmised, we seek the Chain of Chuacar. We have deduced what we believe to be its precise latitude and longitude. Starting tomorrow we will sail north, to the designated latitude, then west until we reach our destination, where we will, I believe, find one of the greatest treasures ever known to man."

"What if it's not there?" Knot asked.

Fish thought that sort of question would've come from Scab, Jumping Jack, or Thimble. But no: the three of them were silent, obedient.

"A perfectly reasonable query. That is, of course, one of the risks of such a quest. There may be no chain, and our journey may prove fruitless. This is why I tell you now. I know at least two boats anchored in the harbor that are in need of able seamen. I hope you will remain with us, but if you wish to leave and join another crew, that choice is yours."

The majority of the crew showed no intention of departing. Yet a dozen men immediately and angrily announced their resignation.

Scab, Jumping Jack, and Thimble were not among these defectors. Scab acted instead like the dutiful mate, bound to his captain's wishes. But his performance — for Fish thought it had to be a performance — was entirely unbelievable.

The captain pointed to the hourglass on the ship's flag. "For those of you who have chosen to remain, I assure you that I understand your time is limited. This is the spirit of the *Scurvy Mistress*, and I will not violate that spirit. We will commit one month to this search, then turn our minds and our swords to more profitable endeavors should it prove fruitless. I say this now to be fair and honest, but I believe that in a short while, we will, each of us, be sleeping on pillows of gold."

The crew passed its last four hours on the island purchasing knives, boots, belts, cutlasses and swords, pistols and muskets. Fish saw Noah haggling over the price of a fiddle, and watched Sammy the Stomach and the Scalawags haul off several gargantuan wheels of hard yellow cheese, cursing and complaining that the store had sold out of salami. The Tea Leaves were frustrated, too; they called the scant selection of tea a capital crime.

Under Foot's eye, Nora replenished the ship's stores of livestock, buying two dozen hens and a pair of fairly mangy goats. Fish was busily attending to a list of his own; Daniel had written out a selection of items and asked his landworthy friend to procure them. He gave Fish enough coins for a new pair of boots, a knife, and any recently published pamphlets on current trends in piracy and navigation. Fish went through the list item by item until he came to the last one: "New shirt for shoeless pirate."

Fish's shirt had been too large to start, and now, after he'd worn it every day for more than two months straight, it was also tattered. Daniel had already done enough for him. But the very notion of a shirt that fit . . . Fish couldn't refuse the gift, either.

In the clothing section of Dolphin Dry Goods, he found Thimble inspecting an enormous pile of multicolored fabrics, tucking a trunk's worth under his arm. Fish successfully avoided him. He found a perfectly sized shirt, tossed his old one aside, and settled his account. Afterward, he rowed back to the ship with three of the Scalawags for Sausage, who were so distraught to leave such fine eateries behind, they actually cried.

For two days, the *Scurvy Mistress* sailed north. Daniel explained that longitude was difficult to determine at sea, so in order to sail to a particular address, they had to place themselves along the right line of latitude first, then sail east or west along that line until crossing the intended line of longitude. From Turtle Island, this meant sailing north, then turning west for several more days before they found their destination.

On the fifth day, a small island appeared in the morning fog as a tall, dark bump. Thick trees grew right to the edge of the narrow sand beach, and there were no indications that the island was inhabited, not even by a goat. Daniel said it looked like it had been lopped off the top of a mountain and dropped into the sea, while Nate thought it was really just an oversized hill. Fish preferred Simon's classification. Since it was neither a mountain nor a hill, Simon declared it to be a mountill.

They approached the island's east side and circled once while Melinda sat on the quarterdeck, busily sketching a map of the land. Fish was eager to see her rendition, but from what he could guess, the island was roughly triangular in shape, with its northernmost point leaning slightly to the east. He wanted to stand with the captain and Melinda as they formulated the plans, but the hierarchy of the ship needed to be respected. He was still a scrub. Only senior pirates were allowed on the quarterdeck at such times.

The *Scurvy Mistress* anchored off the southern shore, the base of the triangle, as the sun faded over the blue-green sea. The crew was quiet that night, more somber than usual. Fish slept little and didn't have the cabbage to blame. He couldn't help wondering if they would find the chain, how long it would take, and whether he would be part of the search. He certainly hoped so.

He was not the only restless sailor. All through the night he could hear Foot grunting, Noah singing quietly to himself, Jack doing his jumping exercises, and plenty of the others moaning and grumbling.

Before dawn a massive boot nudged him in the ribs. He tensed, thinking that Scab was provoking another fight. But it was Moravius, motioning, eyes wide, for Fish to come with him.

He followed the giant into the cabin, where Cobb and Melinda sat, bleary-eyed, at the table. "I found the answer!" Moravius boasted.

"The answer to what?"

The giant pointed to the dozen golden coins. They were spread out, aligned in a row, with the queen's profile facing down. "I discovered the message."

"But these coins are decoys," Fish said. "We already decided on that."

Smiling, Moravius replied, "We were wrong."

"You'll have to excuse him," Cobb said. "He is very proud of himself. He insisted on informing you personally."

"Well, you didn't find the answer, did you, Walter?"

"Tell the boy what you've found, Moravius," Melinda said through a yawn.

He pointed to the letters on the coins, the ones they'd noted that first night in the cabin, when Fish first tried to help. "We know very little about the explorer who first found the chain, Wentworth Collins, the one who left all those clues. But given his name, I had been assuming all along that he was English. And he might very well have been. But we also know he was well traveled, which means he probably would have known other languages, too. So, in thinking this way, I came to realize that the letters were not meant to form an English word at all. See this one?" he said, picking up a coin with the letters *E* and *N*. "I'd been thinking of them as two separate letters, *E* and *N*, but they comprise a single French word."

"A French word?"

"Yes. *En*. Once I realized that, I saw them with unclouded eyes —"

"Tell him!" Cobb shouted.

"Look at the coins," he said, pointing to the first, then pronouncing the letters on each coin in the row. "*R-E-G-A-R-D-E-Z-EN-B-A-S.*"

This meant nothing to Fish.

"*Regardez en bas!*" Moravius exclaimed.

177

Still nothing.

"Must we remind you again that you are the only one of us who speaks French, Moravius?" Cobb said. "Translate, please."

"'Look down!'" the giant said. "It means 'look down.' The first set of coins told us how to find the island, but these tell us where on the island to look. Don't you see? The chain is buried underground!"

"Perhaps in a natural cave," Cobb added.

Moravius began to describe a few more of his theories on the subject, but Cobb dismissed them, declaring that he and his wife needed to ready themselves for the search.

Outside, the sky was turning pink. Moravius took a few deep breaths and crowed like the world's largest, strangest rooster. The men began wandering up, eager to begin. Cobb ordered them to make for shore in the small rowboat, six men at a time, not long after dawn.

Fish took one of the last boats, with Nora, Nate, and Simon. A few members of the crew remained on the *Scurvy Mistress*, including Sammy, Bat, Owl, Thimble, and Daniel. Not even the lure of the legendary golden treasure could coax his friend from that boat. Thimble's choice to remain was odd, though. Fish thought for certain that he would stay with Scab.

On the beach, the crew quickly set up a small camp, gathering wood and stones for a fire and water from a nearby stream. By late morning, Cobb had divided the thirty-odd men into groups of five. He showed them Melinda's rough map and sectioned off the island, assigning each group a different area to scour. Unfortunately, Fish, Nora, and Nate were stuck with Scab and Jumping Jack. They'd been assigned an area to the north, but Scab demanded a switch. "We'll take the southwest corner," he declared, and Cobb saw no reason to protest.

"Why is the search necessary?" Noah asked. "Do you not have some idea of its location?"

"We know it is here," Cobb answered. He opened his arms wide. "As you see, this is not an outlandishly large island, but we are in search of a chain large enough to wrap around the whole of a great city."

Noah removed one of the nails from behind his ear and jabbed it in the air. "Big treasure, small island."

"Precisely. In all likelihood, though, you will not find the chain itself lying on the surface. We have cause to believe that it is buried underground, in a natural cave. You will be searching, naturally, for the entrance."

"And if we find it?" Nate asked.

"Fire two shots. The rest of us will follow the sound and converge there."

Nate leaned over and whispered to Fish. "This is really all we have? No map? No X marks the spot?"

Fish neglected to respond. He was eyeing Scab, who was smiling as if he approved of everything. The smile was unnatural on his scarred, compact face — it looked uncomfortable, too, as though someone were twisting a knife in his back.

The men broke off into their groups. Some proceeded down the beach in either direction; others marched forward into the island's thick brush, hacking at the leaves and bushes with their cutlasses. Fish, Nate, and Nora trailed behind Scab and Jumping Jack. But before they got very far, Cobb called Fish back and gestured toward Scab. "Watch him," he said.

Scab and Jumping Jack, who had donned a hat to keep the sun off his bald head, walked ahead along the shore. When they neared the southwestern point, the first mate stopped. "This is a man's work. We don't know what lies in that brush. You children wait here."

Nate protested.

"That is an order!" Scab barked back.

With that, the two of them disappeared into the trees. Nate bristled, angry at being referred to as a child. He picked up a stone and threw it at a half-submerged boulder. "This is miserable. At least in a raid I get to do something. I don't have to sit around on a beach."

"Perhaps we shouldn't wait," Nora suggested.

Fish quietly watched the brush.

"No," Nate insisted. "He's our superior and he told us to remain on the beach."

"But Fish saw him —"

"No, Fish *smelled* him, and Cobb told him not to be concerned."

Fish kept his voice low and, once he was certain Scab was a good distance away, said, "We're going to follow him."

"What? Not the mutiny again, Fish. Cobb told you —"

"Cobb also told me to watch him."

They tried to follow Scab's trail, but found none. No grass

trampled, no branches or bushes hacked by a cutlass, no twigs snapped underfoot. Furthermore, he could hardly see more than a few paces ahead. He put his nose into the air, searched for a trace of that unique mix of moldy onion and rotting feet, but detected not a hint.

"Forget Scab," Nate said. "How are any of us going to find the entrance to a cave in all this brush?"

"Cobb said we have a month," Nora reminded him. "That should be enough time."

As they moved forward, it became unfortunately, painfully clear that the island was not, in fact, uninhabited. Fish was not sure whether people lived there, but it was certainly home to a very large and vicious population of flies. At first, they were just an occasional nuisance, nipping at his ears and neck. But before long, it was as if those first few flies had buzzed off to invite their friends, neighbors, and distant cousins, who then woke up their mates sleeping in the hills or on the other side of the island, so that they could all swarm around the young pirates' heads.

Yet they pushed on and, hearing voices ahead, followed the sound toward the shore on the western side of the island. They had crossed its southwestern point and were once again close to the water. Fish could smell the sea, and he wanted nothing more than to dive where the flies could not follow him.

But he had to endure the annoyance and find out about those voices. He came to a bush with green leaves as big as his old shirt, crawled forward, and moved a few aside so he could see clear through to the water.

The mystery sloop from Turtle Island lay at anchor a few minutes' swim away. A rowboat rocked in the shore's small waves, and a rough, disheveled bunch stood talking at the water's edge. Scab was among them, along with Jumping Jack and three other pirates he did not recognize. The strangers were predictably ragged. Each one looked like he slept in a pile of mud, ate rotten lobsters without removing the shells, and styled his hair with the slime off a slug's back.

Yet these pirates were not the gravest of his concerns. There were two other figures among them. One was unusually small, and the other was dressed for afternoon tea, not a treasure hunt on a remote island. Reginald and Lady Swift had arrived.

He heard something rustling. A bird flew up out of the brush, startling them. He had to keep calm and think. He could guess why the Swifts were there, but what was their plan? Exactly how did they intend to challenge Cobb for the chain?

Lady Swift was saying something about the coins when another noise distracted him. He expected to see a small furry creature crawling out of the brush, or another bird fluttering toward the sky, but his gaze fell instead on a large pair of black leather boots caked with mud and sand.

A boulderlike man stood over them, aiming one pistol at Fish and swinging the other between Nora and Nate. "Looking for something, children?"

CREEPING
SUPERSTITION

Back on Turtle Island, when Nora and Nate had told Fish about the remarkable creeping ability of Gustavo de Borges, he neglected to ask why such a skill would be useful to a pirate. But now, with each of them bound to tree trunks at the edge of the beach, the answer was obvious.

Fish tried to wrest his hands free, as he had on board the *Scurvy Mistress*, but it was hopeless. Besides, what would he do if he could get loose? Six dirty, stinking rascals stood between him and the sea. There would be no escape. Scab had them now.

Somehow, though, Nate failed to understand their predicament. When Scab stomped up to address them, he sighed, sounding relieved. "Would you please tell these men that we are allies of yours?"

The other pirates laughed. "Allies of mine! Did you hear that?" Scab asked. "And are you allied with Cobb, too?"

"Of course. . . . He is our captain."

"Associates of that overeducated dream chaser are no allies of mine. If you stand with Cobb, you stand against Tenneford the Terrible!"

Fish hadn't heard that name before. "Who is Tenneford the Terrible?"

"I am!" Scab replied angrily.

"But your name is Scab."

"Not anymore. I have not had a scab in years, so that nickname is completely unjustified. I am now to be known as Tenneford the Terrible, and from this day forth I shall haunt the seven seas."

Nora started to giggle. This didn't strike Fish as a very good idea, but the name *was* funny. He couldn't help but smile, too.

Scab stomped over the sand and grabbed Fish by the collar. "You dare laugh at me?"

"We are not laughing at you," Nora answered. "We are laughing at your name, Tenneford. For a pirate, it is terrible."

"My mother gave me that name!"

One of the strangers mumbled, "I told you Terrifying Ten was better. People would think you weren't merely one man, but ten!"

"Tenney the Terror would be an improvement," Gustavo offered.

"Or Captain Terror," offered Jumping Jack.

"Yes," Gustavo agreed, "the simplest ones are often the most fearsome."

"Enough with the names!" said Lady Swift. "And enough with these three pests. I did not sail across an ocean to deal with children. I am here —"

"*We*, mother," Reginald Swift interrupted.

Lady Swift rejected her son's protest. "I repeat, *I* am here for business, not to theorize about names or argue with junior rovers. Scab or Tenneford or whatever you choose to call yourself, may we please hurry along so that I may have my coins and you your ship? Would you dispense with these pests so that we may resume?"

"What does she mean, *your* ship?" Nora asked.

Scab lifted his pistol to Nora's face. "This forehead of yours, so smooth and tall, offers a delightful target," he said.

"No!" Nate shouted.

"Wait!" Fish and Nora added in unison.

"Why should I?"

"Because . . ." Nora began, searching for something convincing to say.

"Because if you fire, Cobb and the others will come running," Fish said.

Scab lowered his weapon. "The minnow is right. We cannot sacrifice our plan for this."

"Then slice open their throats," Lady Swift suggested. "But please wait until your men have rowed us a good way out to the *Mildred*. Much like his minuscule father, my delicate son abhors the sight of blood."

"Mother!"

"Come now, Reginald."

Her tiny son was exasperated. "I see no reason for you to announce the fact! If I'm to assume control of our operation eventually, you must allow me to deal with men of this sort without —"

"Enough!" his mother shouted. "We have treasure to find, people to kill, and you want to talk of the future? If anything, your performance on this disastrous journey has convinced me that I never should have considered you a worthy heir."

Her son's face, a picture of frustration the moment before, now turned a ghastly white. "But you promised. I —"

"Promises! The only fools who keep promises are those who lack the strength to break them. Now please cease speaking unless you are spoken to. Otherwise I'll have one of our hired rascals here wrap one of their filthy bandanas across your all-too-active mouth."

Broken and embarrassed, Reginald Swift did as he was told. Fish thought the small man was one insult away from sobbing.

"Are we finished with the family affairs?" Scab asked. "It's time for us to make our way back to Cobb's camp. Gustavo, you kill them," he ordered. "And once you are done, return to the *Mildred* and wait for my signal."

The signal for what? Fish wondered.

Gustavo raised his cutlass. "Do you mind if I ask again . . . what is the signal?"

"Three pistol shots," Scab replied impatiently.

"Right," Gustavo answered. "And then?"

Though he had a fierce reputation, Gustavo's memory clearly did not match his creeping ability.

"And then you sail the *Mildred* around the coast, move your gear and chests onto the *Scurvy Mistress*, rid her of any unnecessary weight, and take her yourselves. Thimble will dispose of the men; you won't have any trouble boarding her."

That explained why Thimble had remained on board. Scab wasn't interested in the chain. He wanted the *Scurvy Mistress*. But what about the other men? Daniel was on the boat, plus Owl, Bat, and Sammy the Stomach. Fish was certain his friend would try to stop an attempt at mutiny, but he couldn't be sure about the others. He had never said more than a few words to Bat or Owl. And Sammy's only loyalty lay with his vittles.

"You and Jumping Jack are going to handle the rest of Cobb's men?" Gustavo asked.

"No, you fool. I already told you. We have twelve on our side already — in addition to our group here — and we will win more, once I state my case."

Twelve men wasn't a majority, but the numbers weren't encouraging, either.

"Our men will recruit any of the rest who wish to join us," Scab said. "Then we will sink that sorry little sloop, the old hag *Mildred*, and leave Cobb and his loyal flock on the island to die. Understood?"

"Understood," Gustavo answered.

As Scab and Jumping Jack stomped off, Lady Swift walked up to Fish. "You are the messenger boy, the one who was supposed to deliver my coins?"

"I am," Fish said. But for the first time, he didn't regret his failure.

"It isn't entirely your fault, my being forced to sail here aboard a third-rate vessel, like some sort of amateur treasure hunter, and do the work myself instead of happily reclining at my new estate, counting my riches as I'd planned. My incompetent and uniquely small son is, of course, also to blame" — she leaned in close to whisper to him — "but I can't have *him* killed. You, on the other hand . . ."

She touched his cheek with the back of her cold, wrinkled hand, then walked down to the water's edge and climbed into the waiting launch. Over her shoulder she called out to Gustavo: "Save the shoeless one for last. Let him watch his friends die . . . and then kill him slowly." Fish shivered, and Lady Swift changed her tone, becoming almost cheery. "But don't take too long, now. We have a chain to find!"

Fish struggled against the ropes. His skin burned as he tried to free his hands. Gustavo stepped toward him; how that man could have approached them without making a sound he did not know. The necklaces alone should have alerted them. Gustavo was clearly a magician of silence.

Fish should have at least been able to smell him. Though his breath stank more of garlic than onions and rotting feet, it nearly matched Scab's for potency; perhaps that was how the two rogues had become associates in the first place. Maybe they'd sailed together and formed a lunch group consisting of pirates with putrid breath.

Gustavo removed a knife and licked the partially rusted blade. "You know what I like most about being a pirate?" he said. "Murder."

"You're no pirate!" Nate yelled. "You are a coward. A real raider would allow us to fight!"

Gustavo's jaw tightened; Fish could nearly hear his teeth cracking under the strain. Yet he did not answer Nate's challenge. Not with words, at least. Instead, he breathed in deeply through his nose, loosening a clump of something viscous, and spat a mass of green and yellow gloop onto the center of

Nate's forehead. He did the same to Nora, then moved to Fish. He summoned his final phlegmatic shot from his chest, coughing it up into his mouth prior to unloading.

The force of it was incredible. The glob landed in the center of Fish's forehead and stuck there momentarily before sliding gradually down toward the bridge of his nose. If only he could free his hands! Even just one, to wipe that lung-borne slop from his face.

"Don't bother," Gustavo said, watching Fish wriggle. "You've been bound by a knot that only a few people in the world can untie."

No. It couldn't be. Had Gustavo used the Slippery Noodle? Fish had tied and untied the Slippery Noodle on several occasions with Knot's help. But with his wrists tied behind him, he was effectively blind.

Yet he had to try. With the fingers of his right hand he traced the two ends of the rope, felt how they looped in, out, in again, and over. He tried to conjure a picture of the knot in his mind. It definitely felt familiar. But time was short. Gustavo was ready to begin.

The masterful tip-toer spotted the gleam of one of Nora's hidden blades, a small but sharp tool tucked into the cloth she'd tied around her head. He pocketed his rusty weapon, then removed Nora's and held it up to the sun, inspecting the edge. "A perfect knife to kill you with," he said.

Fish quickened his finger work. The knot was loosening, but only slightly. He needed more time.

Gustavo glanced out at his mates, who were rowing the

Swifts back to the ship, then rubbed one of his necklaces, another, and another, closing his eyes as he did so. He caressed them as if they were prayer beads.

The pirate stepped closer, blade out, pointing it from Nora to Nate. "Who would like to bleed first?" he asked.

"Let them go," Nate offered. "Those two are harmless."

"I am not!" Nora protested.

Gustavo rubbed a small green figure hanging from one of his necklaces. Fish stopped working the knot and studied the pirate's jewelry. Those were not prayer beads. They were good luck charms! Charms were common, but most pirates only wore one or two and they often kept them hidden. But the sheer number of Gustavo's charms suggested that this man not only believed in fortune. He was obsessed.

Gustavo moved the blade toward Nate's neck. The boy was breathing heavily. His face had lost its color, and Nora was shouting for Gustavo to stop.

Fish took a breath. This might be his last chance. "It's unlucky, you know."

Gustavo stopped, pulled the knife away from Nate's skin. "Unlucky?" he asked.

"Everyone knows that killing someone under the age of fifteen is bad luck," Fish answered. He tried to sound authoritative.

Gustavo took a step back and faced Fish. "Everyone knows this?"

"Of course," Fish said.

"Absolutely," Nora chimed in, breathless.

"If everyone knows, then why have I never heard word of it before?"

"It is . . . an Italian rule," Fish answered. "Do you speak Italian?"

Gustavo rubbed his chin. "No, I don't. . . ."

"That explains it," Fish said. "Not even Admiral Blood would kill an underage pirate."

"Ha! Blood would kill anyone."

"Anyone over fifteen," Fish responded with certainty. "Otherwise you are cursed with ill fortune for the rest of your life."

"The rest of your life?"

"Or longer," Fish said.

"Longer?"

"Longer," Nora added.

"It's not something a smart pirate does," Nate added, finally joining the conversation.

"You'd be better off leaving us here," Fish said.

"Or freeing us first and then abandoning us," Nate suggested. "That would probably bring you *good* luck."

"Gustavo might not be a scholar," the pirate answered, "but he is no fool!"

Fish glared at Nate. He shouldn't have tried that trick. Gustavo wasn't *that* dumb.

Gustavo began mumbling, shaking his head, rubbing several of the charms around his neck, and kicking the sand. The boat had returned from dropping off Lady Swift, and one of Gustavo's small band was waiting for him to finish.

"So . . ." he said after some thought, "if I leave you here to die, but don't kill you myself, is that bad luck?"

They still had a chance. "No," Fish answered. "Not at all."

"Absolutely not," Nora added.

Gustavo sneered. "Well, then, I hope you rot!"

And with that, he ran to shore, jumped into the boat, and began rowing out to the *Mildred*.

"What now?" Nate asked.

"I can't move my hands, let alone untie the knots," Nora said.

Fish ignored his friends. He was concentrating, renewing his effort with the knot. What had Knot told him? Don't force the Noodle. Pulling too hard on the wrong loop would tighten the whole. The knot had to be coaxed loose, loop by loop. The top layer had two parallel coils, which then disappeared around the bottom; moving back into the center of the knot. He spread the two parallel lines apart, inserting his index finger between them, creating just enough space to reach the intersection. Then he worked on these, reaching in deeper, feeling the whole knot loosen. One of the ends began to slip. He slid his finger through a loop and pulled it free. The first noodle had come loose, and in a few minutes the rest followed. Fish was free.

"H — how did you do it?" Nate stammered.

"Grab one of my blades and cut us loose!" Nora said.

A few moments later, all three of them were free, racing back through the woods. They had to warn Cobb.

TENNEFORD THE TERRIBLE

Back at the camp, Fish, Nate, and Nora crouched behind some bushes at the edge of the beach. All the rest of the men had returned; the mood was anxious yet excited. Fish thought he heard one of the Over and Unders speculating that the missing three must have discovered something, given their absence.

Fish needed to reach Cobb before Scab pounced, but the captain and Melinda were too far away and only a few paces removed from the mutinous first mate.

Pretending to be playful, Scab and Jumping Jack fired their pistols into the air. One shot each, then a third from Scab's other gun. That was their signal. The Swifts, Gustavo, and Scab's crew would be on their way.

Moravius sat removed from the others, with his back to the bushes; Fish, Nate, and Nora would have to alert him instead. They tried whistles, bird calls, even a few little *meow*s, but Moravius didn't hear a thing. With no other choice, Fish tossed a small pebble at his back. It struck its target, but had no effect.

At first Nate and Nora refused to follow his example. They may not have studied *Guidelines for the Enterprising Pirate*, but they'd been around the world enough to know not to anger a giant. "What if he gets mad?" Nate whispered.

"The only person he's going to be angry with is Scab."

They pelted the giant with several small stones. Still nothing. Fish searched the ground, found a slightly larger one, bounced it directly off the back of Moravius's head. The giant spun and saw them.

Though he looked ready to shout, Fish prevented him. He held a finger to his lips with one hand and waved him over with the other.

But they were too late. Scab, having reloaded, calmly pointed one of his pistols at the captain's head and declared that he had a momentous announcement. Jumping Jack aimed two guns at Moravius. Twelve more men drew their weapons and turned them on the rest of the crew, ready to fire should anyone try to challenge Scab.

Scab ordered everyone but his new crew toward the unlit bonfire. Fish panicked and wondered whether they should run, but Moravius gave no indication to Scab that he knew Fish and his friends were hiding nearby. They were safe. For the moment.

Fish felt Nate tense, as if he were ready to charge the beach and challenge the mutineers on his own. He placed a hand on his shoulder and whispered, "Wait. . . ."

"Esteemed rogues, rascals, raiders," Scab said at last, "I am pleased to announce that the *Scurvy Mistress* has a new captain."

"Who?" asked Noah.

"Me, you fool!" Scab shouted. "Colleagues of mine are poised to assume control of her, and from this point forward, she will sail under my command. And as captain, I am hereby declaring an end to these treasure-hunting games. The only real prize within a hundred miles is that wonderful sloop you've been wasting all these years, Cobb, and now I'm going to take her."

Cobb neglected to trace his scar; Fish guessed that, for the captain, violence now seemed like a perfectly appealing solution. His reply had the force of a cannon shot. "YOU WILL NOT STEAL MY BOAT!"

"I already have! Your days as captain are over, and the reign of Tenneford the Terrible has begun!"

Genuinely confused, Cobb asked, "Tenneford the Terrible . . . who is that?"

"I'm Tenneford the Terrible! Don't you remember, Cobb? My name is Tenneford. You're the one who started calling me Scab all those years ago. All because I had a rash. Well, I'm tired of being called Scab, Captain Corn-on-the-cob, and I'm tired of being second in command to a drifting dreamer, and I'm tired of watching a perfect sloop being wasted!"

Cobb rained a series of insults on Scab, calling him a hairless boar, a leprous toe, an encrusted nostril hair, and a lice-ridden scalp, among other things.

Scab ignored the insults and resumed his victory speech. "I may be all these things, but I am also the new captain of that ship," he said, pointing out to sea. "Which means that you crewmen have two choices. Remain here with Cobb or join me and my men as we embark on a pirating adventure the likes of which the oceans have never seen. An adventure," Scab said, pausing before he added the most important point, "that will leave you wealthier than you could ever imagine."

Knot raised his cutlass. Fish hoped he'd remain with Cobb; the man had indirectly saved his life, since he'd taught Fish about the Slippery Noodle.

"Yes, Knot?" Scab asked.

"What about the chain?"

Laughing, Scab shook his head. "Don't you see? Cobb hasn't found the chain, and he isn't going to find it, either."

"But Fish and the others have yet to return. Perhaps they've discovered a clue," Knot suggested.

"All they've found is a date with the devil. They are dead, each of them."

Cobb was shocked. "You've killed them?"

"Yes! They are dead, dead, dead, and if you don't stop interrupting me, you will be, too. I am trying to talk to my men. Hear these words, all of you: You will never find the chain. There is no chain. And that is why I am taking over. I have no desire to waste my best years hunting down an impossible dream. I want to plunder ships! We should conduct ourselves as pirates, not treasure hunters —"

Unprompted, Noah suddenly began to sing:

> *He's not a treasure hunter*
> *No!*
> *He's a pirate through and through.*

Noah stopped as Scab pointed a pistol at his chest. He stomped his foot in the sand, which didn't have the same effect as stomping one's foot on a wooden floor.

"You're not allowed to join us, Noah!" Scab shouted. "Your songs are tiresome! In fact, I declare that there will be no singing at all on my boat."

Several of the men booed, including Jumping Jack.

"Fine," Scab said reluctantly. "If it means so much to you, I will allow some singing. But only after sunset. And only . . . only songs about violence."

"And women?" asked Knot.

"Fine. Women, too," Scab answered. "Now, who else chooses to join me?"

Eight men walked to his side, including Knot and a few of his cronies, the Tea Leaves, who openly admitted that they always sided with whoever held the most weapons, and two Scalawags for Sausage. Thankfully, the One-eyed Willies, Noah, and others remained with Cobb. The captain was not alone, and his remaining crew cheered in his favor.

"We're with Captain Cobb!"

"Tenneford the Tiddlywinker!"

"Toadstool Tenny!"

At least three of Cobb's men declared that they'd miss Noah's singing too much to join Scab. Simon, rubbing his small chin as he devised a new word, announced that he could never ally himself with a rasdrel like Scab.

"Good," Scab said, counting his men. "An ideal crew." In

all, he had eighteen on his side. A dozen stood with Cobb, Melinda, and Moravius.

"And you'll leave the rest of us here to die like dogs?" Cobb asked.

"Yes," he said. "Yes, we will!"

Fish stared out at the water. The *Mildred* would arrive before too long. But for now, at least, Scab did not have control of the *Scurvy Mistress*. If Fish could get there before Scab and alert the men who were loyal to Cobb, then he might be able to stop them.

Quietly, he started to crawl back, deeper into the brush.

"Where are you going?" Nate asked.

"Wait here," Fish said.

"But where are you going?"

"I'm going to swim out to the *Scurvy Mistress* before the *Mildred* can get there. Daniel will help —"

"Scab will get there first."

Of course he would — Fish had completely overlooked this fact.

"I'll stall him," Nate said.

"How?"

"Give me a blade, Nora."

She did, and Nate burst forward onto the beach.

RETURN OF THE DRAGON SLAYER

Fish had to reach the *Scurvy Mistress* undetected, which meant swimming underwater. He slipped into the sea far down the beach, out of sight, pulled on his swimming glasses, sucked in the largest breath of his life, and plunged forward. Before long, his chest ached. He had to breathe eventually, but when the time came, he rose up to the surface, turned to his side, and allowed only his mouth and nose out of the water. A few breaths later he was down again.

When he surfaced at the ship's stern, the *Mildred* had not yet rounded the island's western shore. There was still time. He tied his swimming glasses to his belt, climbed up the rear anchor cable, and crouched on the quarterdeck.

Thimble was up near the bow, watching for the *Mildred*. Yet Daniel was absent. Given that it was daytime, Bat would be sleeping, of course, but normally Daniel would have been sitting watch atop the mast or working on deck. Had Thimble killed him?

Fearing the worst, Fish crept down below, watching Thimble. The pirate failed to notice him. A little more practice, Fish thought, and I'll enter a creeping contest one day.

As expected, Bat and Owl were wrapped in their hammocks, but so were Sammy the Stomach and Daniel. He'd never seen his friend sleep during the day. He grabbed Daniel's shoulder and shook him lightly.

"A sleeping draft," Thimble explained.

Evidently Fish had not been as Gustavo-like as he thought.

"I added it to their breakfast." The raider, gloating, picked up a small brown bottle from a table near Nora's counter. "Purchased it on Turtle Island for this very occasion."

Fish searched for a way out. Could he run past him?

"You won't escape," Thimble said, drawing his cutlass. "But I'm not particularly fond of murder, so why don't we save ourselves the trouble of a mismatched scuffle. Drink what is left in this bottle" — he stepped forward, placed it on the floor, and backed up again — "and you'll enjoy a small nap while we complete our mutiny."

Behind Thimble, Fish spied a trunk overstuffed with fine linens, silks, and spools of thread. He recognized several of the fabrics from Dolphin Dry Goods. Those materials were more precious to Thimble than gold itself. If he could just distract him somehow . . .

Suddenly, Daniel rolled out of his hammock behind Thimble and dropped to the floor. Eyes bleary, he stood up, stiffened, and shouted, "Back, dragon!"

"Daniel, no! Wait!" Fish quickly stepped in front of him. He didn't want his friend to be hurt.

But the sleep-fighter would not be deterred. Cutlass drawn, eyes only half open, Daniel charged toward Thimble. More annoyed than frightened, Thimble dodged out of his path.

Fish saw his chance. He grabbed a match near Meat Pie — the nearest cannon — then raced over to the chest. Fish struck the match and held the flame over Thimble's precious fabrics.

The pirate had sheathed his cutlass and was now aiming a pistol at Daniel.

"Lower your weapon or I will drop it," Fish yelled.

"Extinguish the match or I will extinguish your friend."

This was not the response Fish had hoped for. He had to blow out the flame. But Daniel, still sleeping, suddenly ran at him. Fish leaped away, with Daniel pursuing him.

As Fish fled from his violently dreaming friend, shouting at Daniel to wake up, Thimble began screaming. The fabrics were ablaze. The match! Fish must have dropped it when Daniel charged. Thimble dropped his pistol and dashed across the room. His only concern was saving his precious fabrics.

Fish kicked the pistol out of the way, then ran up to Thimble, grabbed his cutlass, and flung it across the cabin. Surprised, the pirate turned and struck Fish hard across the face.

The man might have been thin, but there was power in that malnourished body. The blow sent Fish spinning to the deck. His cheek burned from the backhanded slap.

Daniel, smelling the smoke from the small fire, mistook Thimble for a monstrous foe: "There you are, dragon!" He jabbed at the trunk with his well-sharpened cutlass. Thimble rolled away, but the boy raced after him. As he dodged

Daniel's strikes, Thimble kept stealing glances at his smoldering fabrics. "Do something, please!" he yelled to Fish. "Those are rare Oriental silks!"

Though Thimble lacked a weapon, Fish feared more for his sleep-fighting friend. Scab's ally would overcome the boy before long. He grabbed a bucket of soapy water and doused Daniel in the middle of a strike. Daniel shook his head and wiped his eyes. For a moment, he looked as though he was about to wake up, but then he yawned, tumbled to the floor, and entered into a far more peaceful sleep.

Thankfully, Thimble didn't bother grabbing the boy's weapon. He raced back to his smoldering fabrics and began splashing them with water.

As long as the pirate was preoccupied, there was still a chance Fish could stop him. But how? A solution appeared in the form of a small brown bottle. He hurried over to where Thimble had placed it on the floor and shook it to confirm that some of the sleeping draft remained. Fish removed Nora's hidden key, snuck into the storeroom, and pulled down an aged bottle of wine from the top shelf. He knew of the red-faced pirate's legendary, uncontrollable thirst for the beverage. Fish could use that against him. He poured out some of the wine and filled it up again with the last of the sleeping potion.

When Fish stepped back out into the room, the pirate was still sorting through the remains of his fabrics. Yet he had also recovered his pistol. He was pointing it at Fish. "You don't have any plans to fight back, do you?"

Fish held up the bottle of the sleeping potion. "On the contrary," he said. "I'd prefer to sleep through the coming battle instead."

"A cowardly choice, as I'd expect from one of Cobb's disciples, but a wise one, too," Thimble answered. His small eyes brightened when he noticed the wine. "And the other bottle?"

"Cobb's reserve vintage, I'm told." Fish held out the bottle. "For you."

"A bribe?"

"An offering. I thought it might convince you to treat me with some leniency."

"I make no guarantees," Thimble answered. "But I accept your offering." He snatched the wine bottle, yanked out the cork with his teeth, spat it aside, and drank greedily.

Then he demanded that the boy do the same. Fish raised the sleeping draft's bottle to his lips and pretended to swill its contents, though not a drop of liquid remained inside.

A pleasure-filled glaze fell over Thimble's red face as he finished the bottle. His tight, hollow cheeks relaxed. His eyes began to close, then sparked open. He was watching Fish now. Suspicious, perhaps. The boy began to feign drowsiness, forcing his eyes nearly shut, but after a moment, this little act proved entirely unnecessary. Thimble dropped to the floor.

Fish dragged the rail-thin pirate into the storeroom, locked the door, and returned Nora's key to its proper place. Still, there was more to be done before he could count himself and his friends victorious. Much more.

He hurried up top and saw the *Mildred* approaching. Back on shore, the launch remained tied in place. None of Scab's men had left yet, and he had not heard any gunfire. Whatever Nate was doing was proving effective. Now it was up to Fish to stop that ship and prevent its crew from boarding. Yet he couldn't not-fight Gustavo and his brutish men. They'd stomp right over him.

So how could he stop them? He thought and thought, then realized he was approaching the question all wrong. You don't stop a boat. You sink it. He had to sink the *Mildred*.

THE STOMACH
FIRES FIRST

The one unmistakable flaw in Fish's decision to sink the enemy sloop was the fact that he had never fired a cannon before. The one time they had fired a gun since he'd been on board, Fish was up on the deck and had not seen any of the process. Oh, how he wished he had read *The Buccaneers' Book of Bombs* or Campbell's *Compendium of Cannons*. Sammy the Stomach, the best gunner on the boat, had offered to loan him both during the trip. Yet Fish had rejected the offers, declaring that he had no interest in weapons.

Then again, Fish did not need the book at all. He had Sammy the Stomach himself. He jumped back down below and found the rotund gunner rolling from side to side beneath his hammock.

"Sammy? Sammy?"

The Stomach didn't answer. Fish shook him and splashed water on his face, but neither tactic proved effective. He couldn't wake the man. Yet he might be able to wake his belly.

Confident that Nora would approve, given the dire circumstances, Fish hastened into the galley, pushed aside several boxes and crates, opened her secret compartment, and took the second half of the salami. Then he hurried back and placed it beneath the gunner's large nostrils.

"Sammy," he said, "I have something for you. . . ."

Sammy's eyes sprang to life, his body and mind suddenly restored by the lure of the salty, fatty meat. He gorged on it, then stood, wobbling. "What happened?" Sammy asked, throwing his hand out against a beam to prevent himself from falling.

"I need your help."

"Get me beer."

Fish filled a huge bowl and brought it back, sloshing and spilling, to Sammy. Immediately the man stood straighter. He grabbed the bowl, drank it all down in one gulp, and let out a horrendous, ship-shaking belch. The smell hit Fish's nose like a fire; the hairs on his arms tingled and he thought he might faint. Sammy the Stomach slapped himself in the face several times, causing his fat cheeks to ripple, then asked again what had happened.

As quickly as he could, leaving out all but the most crucial details, Fish told him about Scab's plan. "We need to fire on the *Mildred* before those men board our ship," he said. "We need to sink her. Can you do that?"

He thought the facts would be enough, but Sammy proved him wrong.

"First tell me why I should stay with Cobb," he said.

Why? Fish hadn't thought of that. Loyalty? Trust? No — if either of those concepts meant anything to Sammy, Fish would not have needed to convince him. Thankfully, Sammy's massive paunch inspired him to concoct a far more convincing argument. "There will be no cook. Nora is staying ashore.

And," he added, "if you choose to help us, I will let you into the storeroom."

The thought of a boat without a cook was too appalling for Sammy to consider, the possibility of devouring anything in the storeroom too attractive to ignore. "I'm with Cobb," he said.

"Can you sink her?"

"Sink her? No, I haven't the guns for that."

Fish appealed to his pride. "But I thought you were the best."

"I am! My appetite and my accuracy know no equals."

"But you can't sink a little sloop?"

Sammy did not answer. Fish pushed open a pair of shutters and watched the *Mildred*, mainsail full, her long bowsprit pointed toward them.

"I suppose, if we were to fire all four on this side — Meat Pie, Zucchini, Sausage One, and Sausage Two — it might be possible. One perfect shot could snap the mast, the other three, placed precisely, could open a large enough hole at the waterline. She'd be crippled at least, if not doomed to the depths."

Fish put his hands on the man's shoulders. "Tell me what to do."

Sammy scrunched his bulbous nose and rubbed his fattened cheeks with vigor. The Stomach was ready to fight. "Fetch eight cartridges from the powder room and bring them here," he said. "And when you're done —"

"Yes?"

"When you're done, get me more beer. I will do the rest."

Sammy was ready when Fish returned. He started ramming the gunpowder-filled cartridges down the necks of his beloved guns. "How far is she?"

"Closing."

Angrily the Stomach shouted back, "I said, '*How far* — '"

Fish estimated the distance. "Two hundred yards."

Sammy stuffed a shot into each of the guns, opened their shutters, then called Fish over to help him roll the cannons forward, so each nose extended out over the water.

"No waves," Sammy said. "No need to account for the roll of the ship in the swells."

The Stomach used a collection of tools to adjust the aim of each gun, lifting the noses and shifting them forward or aft.

"One hundred thirty yards," Fish said.

"I know," Sammy snapped. "Now where's my beer?"

As Fish filled another bowl with brown ale, Sammy walked casually from gun to gun, petting and whispering to them. Then, one by one, starting with Meat Pie, he lit their fuses and tossed the matches into a bucket of water.

The wait felt eternal, but probably amounted to no more than ten seconds. Sammy passed the time in apparent tranquility, leaning against Ham, one of the guns on the starboard side, and gulping his beer.

Meat Pie erupted first. The force of the shot kicked her back toward the middle of the boat, but she stopped midjolt, anchored fast to the deck. Zucchini blasted seconds later, followed instantly by Sausage One and Sausage Two.

Smoke filled the deck, obscuring his view of the *Mildred*. He could hardly see Sammy the Stomach, let alone their target. A series of secondary blasts sounded across the water; one of Sammy's shots must have connected with the *Mildred's* powder room. Fish ran up top to check the results. He cheered and threw a fist in the air. The *Mildred's* mast was cracked near the base and folded over. Her sails were dipping into the sea. Part of the deck had caught fire, and a gaping hole had been opened in the bow. The boat was now pitching forward, swallowing water. It wouldn't be long before she met the bottom.

Though the *Mildred* was doomed, her crew was not ready to capitulate so easily. Gustavo stood at the bow of the sinking ship and began stuffing a cartridge and shot into a small cannon.

This was not part of Fish's plan. He didn't know whether to run, duck, dive overboard, or convince Sammy to loose a few more shots. But at the final, crucial step, Gustavo fumbled his match, dropping it to the deck. And before he could strike another, he was pulled aside.

Lady Swift, her blue dress charred at the base, her gray hair a frazzled mess, stepped in front of the boulderlike pirate. She yelled at him as if he were a child; Fish couldn't hear what she said, but saw Gustavo move obediently out of her way. He was larger and stronger, but the old woman was now in charge of that boat.

She removed a match from a small pocket in her elegant blue dress, struck it against the back of her wrinkled hand,

and set the fuse ablaze. Then she held the match momentarily, letting it burn, while she glared across the water at Fish. She did not speak or shout, but he understood the message. This shot would be for him.

Fish fell to the deck. One . . . two . . . three . . . the shot whistled over his head, punching a hole in a barrel of wine behind him. The deep red drink gushed out, staining his new shirt. Yet he was afraid to move. What if she were to fire again? He waited, then crawled to the railing to see.

The *Mildred*'s bowsprit was now dipping into the water, her stern pointing up at the sun. The cannon was aimed straight into the sea. There would be no more shots.

The *Scurvy Mistress* was quiet. He heard Sammy belch. Their boat was secure, but Fish felt no relief. He still had to deal with Scab and his band of rogues on the beach.

Looking back at the shore, Fish saw that most of the men remained near the bonfire, where he'd seen them last, but the launch was also heading his way. Scab and Jumping Jack sat at the back, each pointing a pair of pistols at Nora and Nate, who were working the oars.

Scab must have determined that something was amiss; the ships were not supposed to fire on each other. He probably concluded that Fish was behind the mayhem and had taken Nora and Nate hostage so that he could —

A musket ball whipped past his ear and struck the mast. He dropped. Where had that come from? Was Thimble free? Off the larboard side he saw Lady Swift standing upon the sinking bow with a brace of pistols hung around her shoulders.

Her gray hair was now swept back, her dress half soaked as if she'd fallen in the water, and she looked angry enough to light that useless cannon with her rage alone.

Her son cowered behind her. Gustavo and his mates were out of the fight; they were busily hoarding their valuables onto the launch, abandoning the ship.

Despite the madness all around her, Lady Swift kept her eyes on Fish, yelling loud enough for him to hear her clearly across the water. "There's no sense hiding, you worthless maggot!" she screamed. "I do not lose! I do not fail! The chain will be mine, and you will die!"

There was only one way to not-fight someone with a collection of ready pistols, whether it was an ill-tempered old lady or a weathered rogue: Run.

And so he did. Then he slipped down into the water on the starboard side of the boat, near the stern. He was out of Lady Swift's range and the *Mildred* was no longer his primary concern; Gustavo and his men wouldn't attempt to board the *Scurvy Mistress* until their possessions were secure. But Scab was moving in fast.

Fish swam toward the bow, staying low to keep from being spotted, and saw the launch approaching. Nate and Nora were doing all the work, rowing hard a few hundred strokes away, urged on by Scab and Jumping Jack. Fish slipped on his swimming glasses and dove.

A good breeze had come up, so the surface was choppy and ragged, but down below the water was clean and clear. He swam beneath the *Scurvy Mistress*, found a rock ledge about thirty yards from the larboard side, and waited. He tried to relax but it proved impossible. His chest was screaming for air; he must have been under for a minute by the time the launch was close enough.

But he couldn't surface just yet. He waited . . . waited . . . reminding himself that his friends' lives depended on him. Not only Nora and Nate, but Daniel, too. Scab would toss Daniel into the sea if Thimble told of his role.

Finally, the boat was overhead. Fish planted his feet on an unusually smooth and flat rock lying below the ledge, on the sea floor, and pushed off toward the surface. He yanked on one of the oars first, pulling it free, then burst out of the water, grabbing the rail of the launch and pulling down hard as he took in a huge breath of air. The boat rocked. Panicked, the pirates stood up, and Fish pulled down on the rail once more.

This time it worked: The rail dropped below the waterline. A small swell rolled in, filling the boat. With a furious cry Scab flew toward Fish, but Nate followed, and the two of them tumbled into the water. The boat flipped, sending Jumping Jack and Nora in after them.

Scab reached for Fish's neck, clamping one hand around his throat, but Fish planted both feet on the pirate's chest and pushed off, breaking free of his grip. Now Fish was out of reach and the rascal was too uncertain in the water to swim after him. With one hand holding the overturned boat, Scab pulled out his cutlass, slashed at the water, and cursed. "Minnow! Squid! I'll roast you, smoke you, boil your bones!"

Nate and Nora were floundering nearby. Fish found one of the oars, had his friends take hold of one end while he pulled the other, and then swam them back to the *Scurvy Mistress*, away from the melee.

A rope ladder dropped down from the deck. They held tight and watched Scab and Jumping Jack, both gripping the overturned launch to stay afloat, drift toward the crippled, sinking *Mildred*.

"Swim over here and fight!" Scab yelled. "Fight like a pirate, you coward!"

His shouts and curses continued, but Fish ceased listening. Let Scab or Tenneford or whatever his name was scream what he liked. He was no concern of theirs any longer. He was floating toward some distant isle. His mutiny was finished.

Nora climbed up first, then Nate. Fish followed, reaching the top exhausted, ready to string up a hammock and collapse for a week. But as soon as he got to his feet, he saw that there would be no rest.

Lady Swift and her son faced the three friends. She was aiming a single pistol their way, and several more were holstered in the brace across her chest.

This fight had to end. Lady Swift had said that she would not fail, but neither would he. Fish would stop this woman.

First, though, he had to delay her. "What about your son? I thought you shielded him from bloodshed," Fish said.

Reginald Swift winced. "I don't need your protection! I can easily cover my own eyes. And if by this comment you mean to imply that my aversion to the sight of blood renders me unfit for —"

"Quiet, Reginald!" Lady Swift said out of the corner of her aged mouth. "A good treasure hunter must do what her predicament demands. And in this case, I must kill you three as quickly as possible, without concern for my diminutive son's gentle nature."

There were no weapons around. Nothing to throw at her. They couldn't charge her, either; she was too far away and she had at least one pistol ready to fire. One of them would be shot. Fish had to stall her further. "How did you get over here? Your ship was sinking."

"The launch," she said, pointing to the starboard side, where they'd thrown up a second ladder to climb up to the deck.

"And the others?" he asked. "Gustavo?"

She held up her free hand, rolling it about her wrist in an uncharacteristically dainty way. "I suppose you could say that I *convinced* them to stay with the ship." Now she aimed the pistol at Fish. "I can be *very* convincing. Now if you will kindly —"

Desperately, Fish shouted, "Wait!"

"Why, so you can concoct a plan to save yourself? No, thank you," she said.

He heard a click, but no report from the pistol.

As she removed another pistol from the brace, the three friends scattered. Nate ducked behind the mast. Fish and Nora took cover behind a large barrel of tack.

Lady Swift saw them move, but she was too busy belittling her son to give chase. "You could have procured weapons that function properly, you incompetent jester!"

"That is hardly my fault! How was I supposed to —"

Ignoring his response, Lady Swift tossed him the stuck weapon, ordered him to reload, and fired her second pistol with success. The shot splintered the barrel edge right beside Nora's ear. She pulled a third gun from the brace, pointed it toward them. How could they stop her? Even Fish's swab was out of reach.

But he had forgotten about his friend's hidden knives. Nora produced a blade from within the confines of her sopping-wet dress and waited for the right moment to throw. Lady Swift's second shot missed wide. She pulled out the fourth and final pistol, but it failed to fire.

Nora jumped out and hurled the knife. Spinning end over end, it missed the aged treasure hunter but pinned her dress to the deck.

Lady Swift struggled and kicked at the bottom of her dress, but the knife was buried too deep in the deck. She was stuck, and promptly blamed her son. "Imbecile! A proper brace of pistols and these rats would be dead! But now look at me! You are like your father. Willing to share in the spoils, but useless in the quest for them!"

"Stop!" Reginald yelled back. "It was not my fault the coins were stolen. It was not my fault our fortune was stolen. And it is not my fault that those pistols did not fire. I am tired of your constant —"

Before Mr. Swift could finish his sentence, Nate swung a plank into his stomach. The tiny man crumpled to the deck, clutching his midsection and moaning.

Next, Nate turned to Lady Swift, who was still pinned by the blade. Fish tried to stop him. Never mind her vicious nature; he didn't want to see his friend strike an old lady.

"No, please, don't hurt me," Lady Swift said, cowering. "I'm merely an old, mad woman. Please! I beg you!"

Nate lowered the plank, and Lady Swift promptly struck him on the side of the head with the butt of her final, jammed pistol. Stunned, he fell backward onto a coil of rope.

Fish rushed to his friend, but Nora charged at the old woman, hurling her fists. Though she might have abandoned her plan to become her father's son, Nora had learned to fight like a man. For his own safety, Fish chose not to intervene.

Lady Swift, pinned in place, had the disadvantage, but she, too, was fierce, landing no shortage of blows to the girl's body. Yet Nora soon overpowered the old woman. After a minute, Lady Swift dropped to the deck, exhausted.

This was no ruse. Lady Swift was defeated, her wrinkled face swelling below her right eye. Fish rushed over with a length of rope and tied the old woman's hands while Nora dislodged her knife, then attended to Nate. She held his hands, gazed into his glassy eyes, and embraced him. Nate emerged from his fog and wrapped his arms around her, too.

"I —" Nate started.

Nora shyly pulled away. "Me, too —"

"Young love, how heartwarming," Lady Swift said with a smirk. "I could say that you will enjoy decades of delightful companionship, but marriage is never delightful and, more importantly, I believe your hours on this earth are rather limited."

Behind him, Fish heard the unsettling click of a pistol being readied to fire.

A Pistol Would
Be Too Quick

Scab was soaked through and angry as a taunted bull. He stuck the tip of his snakelike tongue through one of the hoops in his lip. His dark eyes and thick veins pulsed with hatred. Yet there was a kind of joyful anticipation in his face, too. He was excited, ready to kill.

"H-how —" Fish stammered.

"Up the anchor cable," Scab said proudly. "Isn't that how you boarded my boat the first time? It works well, I'll say. I am not the swimmer you are, of course, but I kept myself afloat long enough to reach it."

With her ally aboard, Lady Swift was revived. "Untie me, you onion-stinking scoundrel!"

"No," Scab replied, "you are far more manageable this way."

Reginald Swift, clutching his stomach, laughed in agreement.

"Reginald!"

"He is correct, Mother."

"In my estimation, Lady Swift, I have fulfilled our terms. Your gold and your coins are both here on the *Scurvy Mistress*. I have reunited you with them, as requested. At the next port, you may disembark with them both, minus the commission of my crew, of course."

Desperation crept into Lady Swift's eyes. "But the chain! We have not even begun —"

"You treasure hunters! You are such fools! I have told Cobb and I will tell you: There is no chain. The *Scurvy Mistress* is mine, and I will waste no more of her time searching for legends. We sail tonight and shall take the first prize we see. In the meantime," he said, pointing his pistol at Fish, "I will dispense with you, you insignificant minnow. And for that task," he said, glancing at his gun, "a weapon of this sort will not do. No, I prefer to see you perish gradually from a thousand small cuts."

With that, Scab tossed his pistol aside and rushed at him.

Fish jumped out of the way, tumbled, and then sprang to his feet. Scab lunged at him again, cutlass drawn. Fish grabbed his swab, held it with both hands, and blocked Scab's blows with the handle. He deflected one aimed at his left side, stepped back, blocked another swinging toward his right, then ducked and felt the metal blade trim the hair atop his head.

Know where you are, Fish reminded himself. Over his shoulder he spotted the puddle of spilled red wine. He backed up, kept his eyes on Scab, and baited the rogue into charging at him. At the last instant, Fish stepped aside and swung his swab at the pirate's ankles. Scab slipped in the puddle and fell to the deck.

But Scab was up again quickly, swinging his blade.

They were too close. Fish couldn't afford to make the same mistake as the last time, trapping himself against a barrel with nowhere to run. If he was going to defeat Scab, he would have to exhaust him. He had to keep moving.

Fish sprinted up to the quarterdeck, dodging a punch to the head and several stabs from the cutlass. Frustrated, Scab threw the blade aside and leaped at him, but Fish was too fast. He ran back down to the deck, then up again, using the handle of the swab as his sword. Fish blocked, ducked, dodged, and dove out of the way as they circled the boat, five, six, seven times. Scab was tiring. Yet the pirate knew how to fight — having thrown his cutlass aside, Scab used other tactics. He stomped on Fish's bare foot up near the bow, crushing his toes, but Fish ignored the pain. He ran for the stern before Scab could take hold of him.

At the top of the stairs to the quarterdeck, the pirate drove his sodden boot into Fish's chest. His balance gone, Fish fell backward, thumped his head, and then rolled down the steps like a barrel. His eyesight blurred. Fish watched Scab coming toward him, but the rogue was shimmering, as if he were underwater. There was a sharp pain in the back of his head and neck, but if Fish remained there, he was finished. *Move!* he told himself. *Move!*

Fish forced himself up and sprinted to the bow, his vision clearing. He not-fought, dashed back to the stern, not-fought some more, then hurried up again to the bow. Scab chased him madly all the while.

Nate aimed a pistol at Scab as the two drew close, but Fish told him not to shoot. This was *his* not-fight. Fish would defeat Scab on his own.

Scab laughed when Fish rejected Nate's help, but his frustration was increasing and his breathing was labored. With every dodged blow Scab grew angrier. His face was now as red as blood.

On the quarterdeck again, Scab grabbed his cutlass and swung at Fish's midsection. Fish held out the swab to block it, but Scab's blade severed the handle and sliced a shallow cut across his stomach. Fish glanced down at the slight wound but remained composed.

The sight of blood renewed Scab's vigor. The pirate swung his cutlass with absolute fury. But Fish knew he could outlast Scab. Fish was not slowed by grog or beer. His legs had not spent two decades at sea.

Scab bulled after him, trying to land kicks to his chest, but Fish was too fast and he only struck air. Soon his thrusts started to become slower and heavier. Scab's breathing grew more and more strained. Even his curses lost their power. "You spineless . . . sardine . . . soft-shell crab . . . slow-swimming . . . sea turtle."

Finally, Scab ceased running and leaned against the mast. He stuck the tip of his cutlass into the deck and leaned on the hilt as if it were a cane. The mate could barely stand.

"Finish him!" Nate yelled. "Finish him or I'll do it myself!"

But Fish had no intention of killing Scab. And he would not allow anyone else to, either. He had backed up against the starboard side of the ship, beside the rope ladder the Swifts had used to climb up onto the deck. The *Mildred*'s launch was directly below him. If he could time it right, it might work.

"You want your ship?" he said to Scab. "You'll have to get rid of me first."

This single, simple taunt was enough. Scab summoned the last of his energy, clenched his leathery fists, and let out a guttural, animal-like roar. He reached into the folds of his shirt, removed a jagged, bloodstained knife, and raced at him.

Fish waited until Scab was merely a step away. Then, just as Daniel had taught him, Fish reached out and clasped the pirate's knife hand, dropped to a crouch as he moved to the side, spun, and pulled the knife toward where his chest had been.

The mutinous pirate, blade extended, was now leaning out over the railing with his knife in thin air, stunned that it hadn't found flesh. Fish moved behind him and, with all his strength, pushed Scab over the edge.

The exhausted pirate landed heavily in the bottom of the launch. He was alive, but barely moving. Fish felt like yelling down to him, "You wanted your own ship? She's all yours." But seeing Scab down there, crumpled, spent, and defeated, was satisfaction enough.

Nate came to his side. "He needs a crew," he said. "Lady Swift, will you descend on your own or must Nora force you?"

Without answering, the old woman stood and held out her tied hands. Nora did her the courtesy of unbinding them and stood by as Lady Swift climbed down into the launch.

Scab hardly registered her arrival; he was only just sitting up.

Fish decided that Thimble belonged with them, too, so he and Nora collected the still-sleeping traitor. On deck, Thimble began to stir. Against Nate's protests, they gave him an armful of his half-burned fabrics, in addition to some water and hardtack for what was sure to be a day or more of drifting. Thimble groggily lowered himself into the boat with Scab and Lady Swift, too tired to resist. And then Fish, as promised, allowed Sammy the Stomach into the storeroom, laughing as the gunner gleefully dug into a brick of cheese.

There was one small matter, though, that Fish, Nate, and Nora had forgotten about. Reginald Swift. He peered down at his mother, then at Fish and his friends.

"Reginald! Get down here now!" his mother called up.

"I intend to stay," he replied. He looked from Fish to Nora to Nate. "If you will allow it."

"Absolutely not!" Nate said.

"Cobb would not approve," Nora added.

"I will do anything," he pleaded. "Anything, so long as I can escape from underneath my mother's thumb. I'll swab the decks, cook . . ."

Anything? Fish wondered. There was one task he'd gladly pass on to someone else, if he could. And he guessed that Nate and Daniel would, too. "Would you scrub the seats of easement?"

Without pause, Reginald Swift, who only hours before had believed himself to be the heir to an immensely profitable treasure-hunting venture, solemnly nodded his head. The most vile task on the boat was preferable to continuing as his mother's minion. "I would and I will."

Fish extended his hand with a smile. "Then welcome to the *Scurvy Mistress*."

"But, Reginald!" Lady Swift cried up to him. "Do you intend to let me drift off into oblivion with these... scoundrels?"

"I worry more for the scoundrels, Mother. You will survive. You always do. But I won't, not if I remain at your arm. Good-bye," he said. "I have excrement to clean."

His mother's apparent desperation faded quickly. "You are just like your father, you tiny fool!"

"Farewell, Mother," he said. Then he looked at Scab and Thimble, and smiled. "Enjoy her company, gentlemen."

Nate threw an arm around the small man's narrow shoulders. "Follow me," he said. "The seats are in a terrible state."

Fish watched Scab closely. He was not one to capitulate easily and, given time to recover from the fall, he would once more be ready to fight for the ship he craved. Scab grabbed the bottom of the ladder, but Nora immediately threw the upper half down on top of him.

Then she pointed the pistol he'd dropped at the erstwhile first mate.

"The oars," she said.

"What about them?"

"Toss them in the water."

Lady Swift protested, "But —"

"Toss them."

Scab was too angry to yell. The whites of his eyes were bloodshot, matching his skin, and a trickle of blood ran down his forehead. Thimble was stirring now, too. He assessed his predicament with clear disappointment.

Lady Swift proved to be as resilient emotionally as she was physically. The defection of her son did not appear to bother her in the slightest. She settled onto her bench, adjusting her damaged dress, and directed Thimble's attention to a more immediate concern. From what Fish could see as they drifted away, Thimble was showing Lady Swift the few fabrics they'd tossed into the boat, intent on mending the charred hem of her otherwise elegant dress.

And no, Scab did not remain silent forever. As the small boat coasted away in the current, drifting one hundred yards, then two hundred, he unleashed a storm of curses and damnations the likes of which Fish had never heard. "You rotten carp! I'll drown you in Cobb's blood! I'll char you over an open fire! I'll use the shards of your broken bones to pick my teeth!"

After a short while, Fish stopped listening to the failed mutineer. The reign of Tenneford the Terrible had come to an end.

Fish climbed up to the quarterdeck, took out a spyglass, and spotted Jumping Jack drifting toward Scab's new ship, clutching an oar. Gustavo and his mates were adrift in the current as well, each holding tight to some broken piece of their former ship. A few of them, Gustavo included, were weeping.

Next he turned and studied the beach. The captain and his wife were standing at the water's edge, staring out at the *Scurvy Mistress*. Moravius loomed behind them, and from what Fish could tell, their former captors were now prisoners themselves, lashed together near the unlit bonfire with a pair of One-eyed Willies guarding them, pistols in hand.

Now, finally, Fish could rest. His friends were safe, their enemies defeated. He sat and stared out at the endless blue sea. He could hear Scab's shouts in the distance, but his curses mingled with the sounds of the wind rushing over the deck, the tiny waves splashing up against the hull. Though it was not his place — or not yet, anyway — Fish was comfortable up there on the quarterdeck, gazing out to sea from his new home.

Forgotten Fish

Yet Fish was not alone for long. Nora and Nate, arms linked, soon joined him on the quarterdeck. Daniel, groggy and slow-footed, followed a few steps behind.

"What happened? What are you three doing here?" Daniel asked. He smelled the smoky traces of cannon fire, stared out at the men drifting off toward the horizon, and then pointed down at the deck, where Reginald Swift was already hard at work, swabbing the area that had been doused with wine after one of his mother's misfires. "What is *he* doing here?" Daniel continued.

Fish rushed forward to embrace his friend. After a moment Daniel pushed away and noticed Fish's ripped shirt. "Your new . . . were you in a fight?" He glanced from Fish to Nate, then Nora. "Would one of you please tell me what's been going on here?"

Nate threw one arm across Fish's back and kept the other linked with Nora. He smiled at Fish, then Nora, and announced, "We've been saving the ship from a mutiny!"

"Scab, Thimble, and more than a dozen others tried to steal the *Scurvy Mistress*," Nora explained. "But we stopped them."

"You three stopped Scab? How?"

"Fish not-fought him to exhaustion!" Nora declared.

Daniel's face was a mixture of admiration and surprise. "You did?! How did I miss —"

"Thimble gave you a sleeping potion," Fish said. "But believe me, you played a crucial role. We could not have done this without you."

Daniel winced and placed a hand to his forehead. "Don't tell me . . . did I sleep-fight again?"

"Like a knight of legend," Fish answered.

"You know, I *did* have some strange dreams. . . ."

The four of them laughed, then Fish stopped and stared once more at the barely visible pirates floating toward the horizon. "We did it," he said to his friends. "We really did it."

Nate pulled at his drenched shirt. "You did get me wet again, though."

"You were the one who dove after Scab!" Fish replied, laughing.

"Dove after —?" Daniel began. "One of you is really going to need to slow down and tell me the whole story."

Nora motioned toward the shore. "First we should tell the captain that his sloop is secure."

"I'll row in," Daniel offered, rubbing his hands. "My head's still full of fog from that sleeping draft. I could use the work."

Nate shook his head. "The launch is gone."

After a pause Nate, Nora, and Daniel all turned to Fish.

"Sure," Fish said, "I'll swim."

Cobb, Melinda, and Moravius did not even wait for him to make it to the sand. They rushed out into the waist-deep water, helped him to his feet, and walked with him up onto the beach. Fish had left his shirt on the boat, and Melinda noticed the cut right away. "Are you hurt?" she asked, leaning in for a closer look. "Who did this?"

"It's nothing," Fish answered, still gathering his breath from the swim. He addressed Cobb: "The *Scurvy Mistress* is safe."

"And the rest of you? Daniel? Nora? Nate?"

"All fine. They are in control now. Bat and Owl are still waking up — Thimble gave them all a sleeping draft — and Sammy the Stomach is attempting to break the buccaneering record for most cheese consumption in a single sitting. We let him into the storeroom as a reward for his work with the cannons."

A few more of the men approached, including Simon and the One-eyed Willies, but Cobb waved them away. "A moment alone, if you will."

When the men turned back, Cobb's face became dark; he traced his scar. "What of Scab?"

"Gone," Fish replied, pointing out to the open sea. "Floating off to who knows where with Jumping Jack, Thimble, and Lady Swift."

"Lady Swift?" Melinda said. "But how did she —"

"She must have been in league with Scab," Cobb cut in. "But she is gone. And so is Scab," he added.

Suddenly joyful, the captain laid his hands on Fish's shoulders. For a moment, he said nothing, merely smiled as he stared at Fish. "All that matters now is the fact that the *Scurvy Mistress* is safe. And we have this young man to thank!"

"You should know that Daniel, Nate, and Nora were instrumental —"

"Of course they were! I would expect nothing less. But you, my boy, you . . ." With his hands still clasping Fish's shoulders, Cobb pulled the boy toward him, embracing Fish. Melinda joined them, too. And then Moravius, unable to restrain himself, stepped forward and wrapped his arms around all three. He lifted them clear off the sand, then grimaced, lowered and released them, holding his shoulder.

"You're hurt?" Fish asked.

"A shot to the shoulder that would have killed a lesser man," Cobb explained. "When the *Scurvy Mistress* fired, Scab and his men turned to see what had happened — I imagine that wasn't part of their plan — so brave Moravius here picked up the log he'd been sitting on, swung it, and knocked nearly a dozen of our former shipmates to the sand."

"Scab fired at him, hitting him in the shoulder, but by that point we'd picked up pistols of our own from the fallen mutineers," Melinda added. "Scab saw no recourse but to take Nora and Nate hostage. He knew we wouldn't risk their lives."

Fish imagined the scene, and the aftermath. "So, since then, you've just been —"

"Waiting!" Cobb said. "The remainder of the cowards dropped their weapons without a fight, but there was no second boat, so we couldn't pursue that treacherous, stinking rogue."

"Noah set to work on constructing a raft, though," Melinda added, "and he should be finished before long."

"I have another assignment for him, too," Cobb said.

"What's that?" Fish asked.

"You'll see soon enough," Cobb answered.

The raft was complete by early afternoon, and the captain rowed out with the first group of four, eager to return to his ship. Cobb had ordered the mutinous pirates lashed to trees along the shore, decreeing that they would remain there, administered water but no food, for two days and two nights as punishment for their treachery. The captain chose not to bind Knot, however; he reasoned that the pirate would extricate himself with ease, so they brought him out to the *Scurvy Mistress* and locked him in the hold.

Cobb ordered a grand celebratory feast. As Nora hurriedly prepared the meal of her young life, using the finest foods on board, the remains of his crew set to work cleaning the deck and constructing a temporary dining area. Noah built a long table made from spare planks, placed it in the middle of the deck, and surrounded it with overturned barrels to serve as stools. Before long the table was piled with charred chops, boiled ham and vegetables, hunks of cheese and fruit, potatoes, and bacon, plus jugs of wine and milk.

Cobb, Melinda, and Moravius sat at one end, with Fish, Nora, Nate, and Daniel across from them. Simon took a spot in the middle, flanked by the One-eyed Willies, and Noah. Bat, Owl, and Foot filled out the other side. Fish had checked on Sammy the Stomach before they began, but the gunner was dead asleep, stupefied from his binge.

The meal was absolutely royal — Fish ate enough for three — and it felt right and good to be enjoying it on the boat. They could have eaten onshore, but after Scab's mutiny, Cobb insisted they celebrate their victory on the *Scurvy Mistress* herself.

Noah stood up from the table, fidgeted with the pencil behind his ear, then clasped his hands behind his back, adjusted his ponytail, and sucked in his potbelly. The captain called for silence, and the carpenter began to sing:

> *He's Fish the swimming pirate,*
> *His first mate is the sea.*
> *Ask that boy to walk the plank*
> *And he'll leap straight off with glee.*
> *Blades might clash*
> *And pistols pop,*
> *His life may be at risk,*
> *But Fish won't swing*
> *A single blade*
> *Nor even raise his fist.*

Noah stopped after those first few lines, swept out his arms and began slowly, signaling the others to join in the chorus:

And . . . he's Fish the swimming pirate,
His first mate is the sea.
Ask that boy to walk the plank
And he'll leap straight off with glee.

They sang two more rounds and each pirate, save Moravius, bellowed louder than the next. When they were done, Fish wasn't sure whether he wanted them to forget the song forever or belt out the chorus just one more time. It felt strange to be hailed a hero. He didn't know how to respond to their smiles and cheers, so he busied himself with a new pile of potatoes.

"Mr. Swift!" Cobb called out afterward. "More libations, if you please!"

The diminutive man hurried over with half a dozen bottles under his arm.

"Wonderful, Mr. Swift. You are doing a very, very fine job. In fact, you may now consider yourself an official member of our esteemed if shorthanded crew."

Reginald Swift abruptly bowed, causing his large glasses to fall to the deck. He placed them back on and bowed again. "I am honored. And I thank you for the compliment, sir," he said.

"The compliment?" Cobb asked.

"I've never had anyone praise my work. I admire the way you lead your crew, Captain Cobb."

"Thank you, Mr. Swift, and you are very welcome. Have you had a chance to sample any of this delightful fare?"

"No," he answered, turning stoic. "The seats of easement require my attention."

As the reborn Reginald Swift hurried off to his duties, Fish struggled to stifle a smile.

Nora, meanwhile, was blushing from Cobb's comment about her meal. "You like the food?"

"It is wonderful, young lady," Cobb said. "We shall have to upgrade your facilities and stores when we find our chain."

Simon, wiping his small chin free of grease with the cuff of his shirt, declared, "It is scrumplicious!"

"That's scrumptious and delicious," Fish whispered to the cook. Then, eager for more details about the day's action, he said aloud, "Your cooking is amazing, but I'd like to hear more about what you did on the beach. How did you two stall Scab?"

"Wasn't I," Nate answered. "Nora proved to be the mastermind."

"What *were* you planning to do, Nate?" she asked.

"I don't know . . . fight them?"

"I assumed as much, which is why I charged out with him, Fish. We weren't going to prevail in a fight. I figured that the only way to slow Scab was to turn his men against him, to discourage them from leaving. So I announced that we'd found the chain."

"A perfect idea, really," Nate added. "Though Scab was suspicious, of course, given the fact that he had ordered one of his men to slice our throats. What were his first words, Nora? '*You should be dead!*'"

"That's right. So we told Scab that we talked Gustavo out of killing us by telling him that it was bad luck to murder young pirates. Scab did believe that part of our story — he knew about Gustavo's obsession with luck."

"But the rest of the men didn't care how we survived," Nate added. "They wanted to know about the chain."

"I told them that we had cut through the woods to get back here faster and that we'd stumbled upon the entrance to a cave," Nora recalled. "I knew you needed time, Fish, so I described, at length —"

"At great length," Nate added.

"I described at *great* length what we'd supposedly seen," she continued. "I invented a small tale about an underground cave —"

"The cave was a fabrication, too?" Noah asked.

"Of course it was!" Nate replied.

The group laughed at Noah's gullibility.

"We told them that you were at the cave, marking the entrance, waiting for us to return. Scab still didn't believe us, but the men were convinced," Nora resumed. "They could all but smell the gold."

"Rushing into Scab's life of raiding suddenly wasn't so important once they believed the chain was nearby," Nate said. "They didn't want to leave the island until they'd searched that cave."

"Scab tried to convince them that we were lying," Nora added, "but they wanted to see for themselves. If he had tried to make those men leave, he would have had a mutiny on his hands."

"Tenneford the Terrible's first lesson in leadership." Cobb laughed.

"I really did believe you, Nora," Noah added, pointing his pencil at her. "I started penning a song about you, though I've since forgotten the chorus."

Fish caught Moravius elbowing Cobb.

"I believed you, too," the captain admitted. "And I do still believe we will find it! But please, proceed with your story."

"The men were eager to go looking for the chain themselves, and Scab looked ready to leave them behind, when we heard the *Scurvy Mistress* fire," Nora said. "Scab knew right away that something had gone wrong."

Daniel raised a forkful of pork to interrupt. "And that's when Moravius took over?" he asked, having heard bits of the story already.

Nate jumped up from the table and acted out the next portion. "Before Scab could respond, Moravius swung that log as if it were light as a swab and felled a dozen of those dastardly turncoats."

Moravius replied with a modified bow and winced from the movement.

"Hence the wound," Cobb noted.

"Then Scab and Jumping Jack grabbed us and forced us to row them out to the *Scurvy Mistress*," Nate added.

"But Tenneford the Terrible never expected Fish to strike from below!" Melinda said.

The group cheered again and raised their mugs, but Fish did not join them. Melinda's words brought him back down below the surface, to the moment before he swam up beneath Scab's boat. The pain in his chest returned, as if he were still holding his breath, and he recalled an observation he'd made at the time. It wasn't even a full thought, really, just something odd he'd noticed about the rock he'd pushed off of to swim up toward the boat. He recalled, in that instant, being surprised that it felt so smooth and flat, almost as if it were polished. Could that have been —

He shot to his feet, nearly upending the makeshift table.

"What is it?" Cobb asked.

"The gold coins," Fish blurted, almost too excited to speak. "Where are they?"

"In my cabin, of course."

Without asking permission, Fish hurried away from the table and made straight for the captain's quarters. The rest of the group followed, crowding inside. Fish spread the remaining coins, the ones with that message in French, across the table.

"What is it?" Cobb asked. "What have you found?"

"The shiny coins," Fish said. "The golden ones that told us to look down."

Moravius started to reply, then caught himself and coughed.

"Regardez en bas," Melinda said.

"What of them?" Cobb asked.

Fish held one out to Cobb and tossed a few more to the others in the room, including Nate, Daniel, Nora, Melinda, and Simon. "What do you see?"

"Letters," Nate said.

Nora shrugged. "Leaves?"

"And fish," Daniel added.

"Exactly! Fish! Don't you see? *Look down!*"

"I don't understand," Cobb said.

Now Melinda jumped in. "You don't think —"

"What if the chain is not on the island at all?" Fish asked. "What if we're not *looking down* in the right place?"

Cobb pointed at the swimming glasses tied to Fish's belt. "There is only one way to find the answer."

Fish needed no further instructions. Seconds later, he was back in the water, fixing his glasses over his eyes and preparing for a dive. He tried to guess where he'd positioned himself before so that he might locate the same ledge and the same strangely smooth and flat rock. But if his theory was correct, what he was searching for wouldn't be all that difficult to find. He wouldn't need to be in a precise spot.

Beneath the surface, he saw a long line of identically sized and shaped rocks extending far in either direction. The arrangement was unnatural. The line was only interrupted where the sunken *Mildred* had settled down to the floor. Otherwise it wove between the beds and branches of coral as if every piece had been purposefully placed. Each of the strange rocks looked to be linked to the next.

He kicked down to the bottom, swept the sand off one of the stones. Right there, beneath him, lay a block of gold as large as Sammy the Stomach's massive paunch. Clusters of sea grass grew on and around it, but he was sure it was gold. He tore off the greenery and saw that it was encrusted with blue and purple stones. He turned in one direction, then the other. This was no trick of the light. This was no illusion. Large bejeweled blocks of gold wrapped around the whole of the island like a chain around some giant queen's neck. He had found the Chain of Chuacar.

His starved lungs were screaming for air, but he couldn't kick back to the surface. Not right away. For at least a moment more, before he swam up to tell the others, he would stay down there, at the bottom of the sea, alone with his discovery. This was where he belonged. He was no farmer. He was no messenger boy. He was Fish, a treasure hunter.

An Unexpected Visit

Fergal Reidy was hacking at the black soil, working the farm's northernmost field, when he saw his son Conor come running. There was no panic in the boy's eyes, no fear. Instead, the boy looked happy — a rare emotion in the Reidy household given the long, hard days, the coming winter, the terrible scarcity of food.

He grunted at his son.

"Come, Father! You must come and see!"

Another grunt. "What is it?"

"It's Uncle Gerry."

"And Fish?" he asked quietly. They'd heard nothing of the boy for months and received no funds since early spring. Fergal had decided he would have to journey to the city soon to see what had become of him, but as of yet he had not been able. He could not miss a day in the field.

"You'll see," Conor said, smiling.

The boy ran back toward their home. Fergal followed him, walking faster than usual, and found his brother outside with Brigid and the rest of the children. His wife, too, was smiling. Gerry pointed to the horse and grunted.

"Ours?"

"Yes, yours."

"And these, too, Father!" Michael yelled, pointing to the

small, fallow field on the other side of the cottage, where eleven more healthy, good-sized mares were grazing.

Fergal didn't understand. He grunted, then grunted again. A dozen horses? Why was his brother giving him a dozen horses? "And what of my son? Where is Fish? Where is Maurice?"

Gerry held out a large black satchel. Fergal took it and nearly dropped it from the weight. Inside there were countless bright golden coins. "What is all this? Where is my son? Where is Fish?" He looked at his wife, but Brigid's face held no answers.

"This is all a gift from your son, Fergal," Gerry told him. "The horses and the gold."

"What do you mean? How can that be? He's only a boy."

"Let's go for a walk, shall we? There are a few matters about your son, and the new career he has chosen, that we need to discuss."

ACKNOWLEDGMENTS

Nika, for love, friendship, sanity, faith, and so much more. Clare and Elle! Mom and Dad, for overt and covert support. Maurice and Brigid. Pops and Nina. The early readers: Ms. Thayer, Rex, Nick, Celeste, James, Charlie, Lawler, Big Mo, and the incomparable Joaquim Pedro. Pools, oceans, waves, the Long Island Sound. The Hungarian table, Valentina, Aldo's coffee. The DA and Kemper Donovan at Circle of Confusion, for dabbling in books and finding *Fish* a home. Adam Rau, for insightful input, Phil Falco for excellent design, Jake Parker for fantastic cover art, and David Saylor, for dedication, countless reads, passion, and all-around editorial guidance.

ABOUT THE AUTHOR

Gregory Mone comes from an Irish-American family of swimmers and storytellers. There were no pirates in the family, but some details in *Fish* were borrowed from family history. Maurice "Fish" Reidy was named for Gregory's grandfather, and though the real Maurice wasn't much of a swimmer, he did cross the ocean on a boat when he immigrated to the United States from Ireland. Gregory's grandmother, Brigid, was forced to leave her family farm when their horse, Shamrock, died. She, too, came to America and, like Fish, had to send money back home to support her family.

The idea for *Fish* sprang from family summers spent with Gregory's nieces and nephews on Long Island's north shore. Setting up elaborate treasure hunts became the day's entertainment. After one such adventure with a map and clues leading to a sunken treasure, the children asked their uncle to write a pirate story.

A Contributing Editor at *Popular Science* magazine, Gregory has written articles about intelligent robots, Irish mythology, cartoons, and alternative energy for many publications. He is also the author of two previous books for adults, *The Wages of Genius* and *The Truth About Santa: Wormholes, Robots, and What Really Happens on Christmas Eve*. Gregory enjoys surfing and was a nationally ranked competitive swimmer.

He lives in Canton, Massachusetts, with his wife and two daughters.

This book was edited by David Saylor and designed by Phil Falco. The text was set in Adobe Garamond, a typeface designed by Robert Slimback in 1989. The display type was set in Clarendon, designed by Robert Besley in 1845. The book was typeset at NK Graphics and printed and bound at R. R. Donnelley in Crawfordsville, Indiana. The production was supervised by Joy Simpkins. The manufacturing was overseen by Jess White.